whiskey business

WILLOW SANDERS

Edited By: Amy Briggs, Briggs Consulting, LLC
Cover Design: Cormar Covers

for jasper

Now you know of AT LEAST ONE romance novel with an
Indian main male character.

one

Remle.

There's a reason I don't drink bourbon. Not being a fan of the taste of spirits aside, I can't hold my booze. My poor, sheltered soul, who attended a party school *for the sports teams*, had literally *zero* alcohol tolerance. None. For the first thirty-five years of my life, this had no bearing on my existence. Everything changed the day I was told to drive myself to Sycamore Mountain and meet with Jasper Raj.

That man. His name should be filed into the *Oxford Dictionary* under "misanthrope," "recluse," and, "arrogant know it all." Oh. Also, hot as butter on a fresh biscuit. No one should be so gorgeous, yet so unfriendly.

I'd been working for the National Bourbon Association since graduating from college. I'd worked my way up from a membership coordinator, eventually landing a job as the public relations director. This year, my task for National Bourbon Day was to reach out to distilleries in other states. Kentucky had a reputation for being exclusionary in what "deserved" to be called bourbon, and my task was to change the mindset and highlight some of our partners who were outside Kentucky.

I needed something big to underline the fact the name bourbon represented *what was in it* more than where it was distilled. The one thing I could use to heighten visibility was the exclusive and elusive Lakshmi Distillery. Distilled in Sycamore Mountain, North Carolina, their limited edition, special label bourbon would make the perfect poster child for out-of-state success stories.

Of course, Lakshmi wasn't an NBA member. Even worse, the owner, Jasper Raj, had a reputation for being distant, inaccessible, and thoroughly disinterested in promotion, marketing, or really anything to expand the distribution of his bottles. If I wasn't responsible for selling the benefits of being part of the association, I could respect his choice. Having a product so selective they distilled it only for special clients made it even more desirable; people fell over themselves for a chance to buy up his bottles the moment the barrels opened.

My tasks were simple. Get to North Carolina. Find Jasper Raj. Convince him to join the NBA and agree to allow us to promote him. What could go wrong?

The answer? Lots. This sudden pivot in strategy arrived at the zero hour. It wasn't any stroke of marketing genius, the desire for deep root engagement, or strengthening our bench outside of Kentucky. It came down to money and memberships. We'd already tapped into all the distilleries in Kentucky. Nothing new ever popped up because the large distilleries cornered the market and made it pretty impossible for the little guys. With membership stagnating, the old guard of stuffy, white-bearded, cigar smoking, good old boys finally deigned to consider we may need fresh blood in the association if we wanted it to survive.

After months of debating what exactly constituted a bourbon, those good old boys finally walked back their assertions bourbon had to be distilled in Kentucky. So long as it was fifty-one percent corn, used fermented grain, and aged in new barrels made from white oak trees, they considered it bourbon.

What state has a large population of white oak trees, especially up in the mountains? North Carolina. Specifically, Sycamore Mountain.

So many, in fact, the charming town inn bore the name The White Oak Inn. It would be my home until I could convince Jasper to sign Lakshmi on to the NBA. If I believed it, I could achieve it. Hopefully, before June fourteenth.

Sycamore Mountain.

two

Jasper

I never expected to find such peace in Sycamore
Mountain. It was a total divergence from the
trajectory of my life. I'd studied hard, and gotten into
top tier schools, including John Hopkins for Medical School,
where everyone wanted to have residency. I held sub-
specialties in three areas by the time I was thirty. By thirty-
five, I held an attending physicianship at one of the most
prestigious hospitals in the country.

I pushed myself hard. I was so hyper-focused on my
personal success metrics I'd forgotten exactly why I did it.
Both my sister and I went to medical school and fed
ourselves into the grinder of the high stakes medicine
within the E.R. Her in Los Angeles, me in Chicago—we were
the perfect Indian children providing our parents plenty of
fodder to brag about with the uncles and aunties.

Now all the pressures of being the dutiful child fell on
my sister, Meera. Not sorry. The specifics were not
important. Simply put, medicine no longer held the appeal
it once did.

I'd stumbled upon brewing. My college roommate at Northwestern, Patterson, we called him Pat, hailed from Kentucky. He came from old horse racing money, and his uncle had expanded the family fortune into bourbon distilling. I'd never realized how much I picked up spending time with them in the summers. When one of my medical colleagues offered me his winter cabin to step away from medicine for a while, the perfect location for a distilling barn cropped up and suddenly I was turning in my resignation and beginning again.

Distilling was peaceful. Quiet. It allowed me to do my thing without a thousand crises happening at once and needing to be triaged. No decisions needed to be made within the nucleus of a second. And, any mistake made, any overcompensation or misstep could be corrected through the process—or someone could simply toss a bad batch out and start over. Nothing was life or death. Simplicity. Peace. All the things I craved.

Until, of course, the day Remle Clay waltzed into my life. Waltz is the wrong word. She lifted a pretty manicured fingernail to my serene bubble and popped it open. All while flashing me a sweet as pie smile made up of the most perfect set of pearly whites, framed with made-for-sinning red lipstick.

three
Remle.

Sycamore Mountain couldn't be more picturesque if someone kidnapped Thomas Kincaid and forced him to design his ideal imagination around town. The White Oak Inn was a charming, white clapboard rambling two story with a freaking tree swing on the front lawn and cutesy sign on the door that read "White Oak Inn, where you enter as strangers and leave as friends."

"Good morning, sugar!" Betty White's younger southern sister greeted me as soon as the tinkling bell on the door announced my arrival. "You must be Remle Clay."

"I am!" I laughed, dragging my rolling suitcase alongside me and setting my tote on top of it.

"We don't get many Monday check-ins." Betty White's sister—named Iris, according to the sign on the desk—explained. "You here for pleasure?"

"No." I chuckled, digging out my credit card and driver's license. "Business. I need to call on Jasper Raj at Lakshmi."

Iris cocked her head to the side, one hand resting against her hip and the other one resting on the counter. "I wouldn't have thought Mr. Hermit even owned a telephone, let alone did things right and proper, like holding business meetings."

At least I wasn't the only one who couldn't get anyone to pick up a phone up there. I'd tried calling him at least fifteen times. My emails, tweets, DM's to his Instagram, all went unanswered.

"Oh, I don't have an appointment. It's more a last-ditch attempt to contact."

"Are you sure you want to stay the whole week, then?" Iris asked, handing me my key. "I'd say your visit is going to be much shorter than you anticipate. He doesn't take kindly to strangers."

I knew this. The guy was a total quagmire. He had literally no digital footprint. Not a single social media account, no news articles prior to Lakshmi really taking off four years ago. Even his Wikipedia and Google pages left much to be desired. His company website listed a single employee by the name of Meadow. I'd tried her email a hundred times as well. She didn't reply.

"Is there a shop in town where I could buy a gift? Maybe some cookies or any type of gift basket?" I asked Iris, collecting my key and my bags.

"Well, Honey Bunz is the local bakery. Aiden, the owner, is such a flirt. He'll definitely make you blush, but don't get your hopes up. He's spoken for!"

As if I had any interest in dating someone in Sycamore Mountain, North Carolina. Not that there was anything wrong with small mountain towns, but I had zero interest in a long-distance relationship. Even if it was only five hours to Lexington from here.

"I'm not interested in any romance, Iris. I'm here to get

7

Mr. Raj to sign on the dotted line, and then I'll be on my merry way."

She looked at me with her eyebrow raised but said nothing more about this Aiden fellow.

"Finley's Market has some real fancy things there, too. It's too rich for my blood but the youngins like it. You know the professional ones. I think they call them Millennials. It's popular with them folk. But I've seen people walk out of there with packages all done up in cellophane. They're over on Larch Street. You'll probably pass by it before you get to Honey Bunz, which is on Main Street."

She had little tri-fold flyers on display to the left of her check-in counter. I watched her carefully sort through each stack before taking a few and handing them to me.

"Lakshmi is up the mountain on Tumbling Ridge. You'll pass through McIntyre Meadow and around the bend and then swing down by the river. There's a little watermill and a sign with fancy writing called Sanskrit. If you blink, you'll drive right past it, so look out for the watermill."

Iris would be my best asset this week. Chatty women like her knew everyone and everything.

"Thank you for all of your help, Iris! Here's my phone number." I wrote it out on the registration slip she asked me to sign. "If you need anything while I'm out, cup of coffee or a magazine—you let me know and I'll be happy to grab it."

She blushed clear up to where her snow-white hair swooped away from her forehead.

"Now don't be silly. I have a perfectly good coffee maker right here. Go on and enjoy the town. We've got charm in spades!"

She shooed me past the counter and toward the rooms. I

may have disappointed her just a bit when all I did was drop my luggage, turn, and head back out. I promised myself I'd take a moment to appreciate her furnishings when I returned.

"Now, if you don't look like a breath of fresh air after a rain shower, I don't know what does."

Aiden, I assumed, greeted me as I stepped into Honey Bunz. Finley's had fancy baskets and such, but nothing really said "you and I would make a great partnership" without looking boring and stuffy. I wanted something charming. Sweet. Something that would bring a smile to someone's face.

"You must be Aiden." I extended my hand across his counter. "Iris warned me about you. I'm Remle Clay."

"She warned you?" His eyes widened, and he pointed at himself in total shock.

"I've heard you can charm the venom out of a snake."

He laughed, wiping his hands on a towel draped over his shoulder before turning back to his very complex coffee machine.

"What can I get you Remle Clay, sweet confidant to the lovely Iris, and looking as fresh as a spring meadow in that dress of yours?"

The guy had charm for days.

"It's a good thing you're head over heels for Cece," a woman stepped up, playfully shoving him with her shoulder, "because you are a total, incurable flirt."

"I'll try your honey vanilla latte, and also can I get a half dozen of your honey lavender scones?"

Addison, according to her nametag, turned and headed toward the pastry display while Aiden took to making my latte.

"Oh, do you have like a pretty box or some kind of fancy packaging to put those in?"

Addison held up two boxes, and I'd been about to tell her I liked both when my phone lit up.

"Hey, Shep!"

Shepard Estes. A bow tie wearing, bourbon sipping, virtue signaling, social climber who spent more time bragging about the cost of his per person charity galas than he spent actually paying attention to any pressing issues affecting Lexington. He was also my boss. Though boss is a loose term for someone who prefers to "entertain clients" over bourbon and cigars.

I greeted him with a smile I didn't feel. This whole panicked accrual of new members had been his idea and ever since he'd spoken it into the universe, he sat on his idea like the first hatching spring duck. Honestly, my mom should cut him a check for his impressive babysitting.

"Remle, what's the status of this Raj guy?"

"Shep, it's literally," I pulled my phone away from my ear to check the time, "ten forty-five. I just arrived forty minutes ago. I haven't even *seen* Jasper yet, let alone had time to pitch him."

He huffed into the phone. And not just like a normal pattern of breathing huff, but the kind which was noisy and sounded... wet. I wanted to believe he wasn't already hitting the drinking clubs, but who knew?

"Honey vanilla latte! Order up!" Aiden called from only three feet away, a devilish smile on his lips.

"The last time I checked," Shep continued, "Jasper Raj owns a distillery. Not a coffee shop. I want an update by one o'clock. It best come with a contract attached."

He disconnected before I could say anything else. I tossed my phone into my purse with an annoyed sigh and pulled out my wallet. *Prick.*

"Eleven oh seven." Addison placed the sweetly wrapped box of scones in front of me next to my latte.

"I couldn't help but overhear," Aiden leaned against the counter, watching Addison put my scones in a bag and dole out change, "you're meeting with the infamous Jasper Raj?"

"Well, meeting with him is a stretch. More like trying to bribe him to give me ten minutes of his time with these lovely scones and my sparkling personality."

"Stop it!" Aiden laughed. "Please, may I come with you? I need to see this. You cold calling Jasper Raj might be the best entertainment we have had up here for months."

He turned to Addison, laughing. "Maybe we should give her the day-old discounted baked goods. It's not like he's going to eat them anyway. Then we can save her six dollars."

"He can't be that bad?" I hedged, trying to keep my confidence up.

"Bad is the wrong word." Addison's rounded eyes broadcast a level of sympathy which truly had me worried about what would happen when I came face to face with Jasper. "He's just... not really social. Jasper likes to keep to himself. He's an enigma around here. I've only spoken with him like a handful of times in the five years he's lived here."

"His assistant Meadow is super tight lipped about him.

We all think he made her sign some kind of NDA," Aiden chimed in.

"Like a *Fifty Shades of Grey* kind of NDA," Addison chirped, hiding her snicker behind her hand.

"Stop it Addy. You're terrible." Aiden chuckled, looking toward me again. "No one really sees much of him. Meadow does most of his errand running, and on the occasion when he is in town, his interactions are pretty limited. He's not very chatty and honestly you kind of forget he exists until one day he walks in and you're like," Aiden opened his eyes super wide and dropped his jaw into a surprised "O." He spent a few seconds continuing to pantomime his shock while also crafting an order for the ghost of Jasper Raj.

"I don't think I've ever even heard him make a comment about the weather."

"Of course, it could just be he's really shy," Addison interjected. "I mean—it's been five years now, so hopefully he's not still shy around the townies. Regardless, though, it's hard to get him to want to talk to anyone."

"Well," I collected the scones and my coffee, "I'm headed there now, so wish me luck."

They both waved at me and smiled. As I pushed through the front door of Honey Bunz, I heard them calling their well wishes over my shoulder. Jasper couldn't possibly be that bad, could he?

four

Jasper

If someone would have told me ten years ago one day in the future I'd walk away from a lucrative attending physicianship, sell my high rise, and find some kind of inner peace in the mountains, I would have arrogantly pulled out the little pad I carried in my breast pocket and ordered them to be remanded under a 5150 for psychosis. Ten years ago, I rode high on my success. It wasn't until eight years ago my arrogance would be my downfall. Seven years ago, my friend offered me a mountain retreat to clear my head and refocus my priorities and six years ago, I barreled my first bourbon whiskey.

Lakshmi was still very young by distilling standards. We'd been distilling every six months, and in very small quantities. I first thought our youth and six-month bottle schedule would be our downfall. Less access to product, struggling with trying to keep up with demands like the big distillers. But what we found was a niche market of wealthy millennials who wanted something not everyone had. They'd pay extra to be able to say only ninety-nine other people could enjoy the bottle they did. Soon after, I had celebrities from Snoop Dogg to politicians asking for special label bottles. We were elusive. That, apparently, made us super successful.

"J.R.! You might want to come see this."

Meadow, my "girl Friday," and all-around queen of my business, shouted to me from the tasting room. While she was fairly young, early thirties max, she had binged old episodes of *Dallas* at some point and thought it was hilarious to call me "J.R." Despite us being in the *sipping* spirits, she liked to say I was the J.R. who sold the shots instead of taking the shot.

I distilled, sold, held meetings, and did everything pertaining to my business steps from where I lived. It made life easier. Being able to just walk out to the barns during the mashing process was so much simpler when I live just upstairs.

Meadow and I tended to the handling our administrative tasks from the tasting room. The table was long and wide, the floor to ceiling windows looked out over the river and mountains, and the chairs were comfortably stuffed. The whole atmosphere made doing tedious tasks so much more pleasant.

I met Meadow at the windows in the tasting room, ready to make some smart assed comment about her neediness. A woman with a lion's mane of burnished sunset hair and a serpentine figure sauntered up our driveway with the most ostentatious gift basket in her hands. As if that wasn't enough of a sight, she wore oversized Jackie O sunglasses, a curve hugging dress in the most fetching shade of grass green, and a pair of heels which screamed "my idea of the country is a lake front cabin somewhere."

"Meadow, what—or rather, who—is on my calendar today?"

I knew the answer. She and I had an unspoken rule. I took zero unsolicited meetings. None. Meadow was hired to be my gatekeeper, my fly swatter, and every other euphemism for keeping pain in the ass salespeople out of my hair. I'd dealt with too many shit eaters as an M.D. All of them with their perfect, straight white teeth, and sleek hair, designer clothes, and cheerleader level enthusiasm. I didn't want to be sold anything. I knew what I liked and wanted. What I didn't like was wasting my time in useless meetings trying to be convinced I needed whatever hot new thing they were insistent I wouldn't survive without.

"There is nothing on your calendar today, J.R."

She drew out the word "nothing" with a sassy little attitude. As if I'd told her the jeans she presently wore made her ass look big. She and I were cut from the same cloth. Meadow, without a doubt, was a high achiever. Any time I even *suggested* something was *potentially* overlooked, she took it as a personal insult. It was probably the reason she somehow ingratiated herself into my confidences over the years.

The two of us gawked while the red head closed the last few feet to the front door.

"Not it!" I whispered, ducking into my office and shutting the door.

"You must be Meadow!" I could hear her soft southern accent even behind my closed door. She definitely wasn't a Carolinian. "I'm Remle Clay, NBA."

Meadow's voice was in direct contrast to Ms. Clay. I had to strain to hear even the vibrations of her voice.

15

"I totally understand. But I was in the area and figured I'd just drop by and introduce myself."

Remle continued, still at a volume better suited for an old person's home.

"Is Mr. Raj in?" She pressed. "I only need like five minutes of his time. Really, just to give him a little token of our appreciation from the Bourbon Association."

I felt my eyes roll unbidden.

"Bourbon Association?" Meadow pressed. "Funny, I thought Kentucky had its arms *very* firmly around who could and couldn't call themselves bourbon."

"Well, from my research," Remle continued with a disingenuous sing-songy voice, "Lakshmi is made of fifty-five percent corn, which is above industry standard for bourbon."

At least she pronounced Lakshmi right. The people of Sycamore Mountain pronounced it *lack-sh-me* instead of *lock-shmee*. Silence hung in the air for so long I thought Remle left.

"Here it is." I heard Meadow's voice rise with triumph. "Mr. Raj, this letter is to inform you *despite* Lakshmi meeting industry standards for mash ratios and barreling procedures, it is with regret that per the requirements of the National Bourbon Association, your distillery resides outside the boundaries of what is considered bourbon territory and you will need to remove the reference to *bourbon* from all of your packaging."

I would admit without shame I'd gone from casually listening to their conversation to gluttonously devouring it. Meadow was savage. While I gleefully hid behind my door like a chicken, she verbally dressed down the smiley rep from the NBA with receipts.

"I guess then, according to the NBA's own assertions, we are in fact a *whiskey* business. Which, of course, means we aren't really interested in anything the NBA has to offer. But thanks for stopping by. I'll be sure to pass on your regards to Mr. Raj when he returns."

Whatever Remle said, I didn't hear. It must have signaled her white-flagged retreat. A few moments later, I heard the subtle ding of the door sensor. The windows in my office didn't afford the same unobstructed view of the driveway, but I could see enough. Like her hair getting caught in a gust of wind just as she went to fold herself into her economy, compact car. She sat in my driveway for a good five minutes. I desperately wanted to know what she was doing, but I was too far away to see anything in detail.

"You are free to roam about the office." The clicking of the door handle as Meadow yanked on it and pushed open the door, jolted me.

"Jesus, Meadow, you nearly sent me to the angels."

"Please. Like any angel would take you without a few months sweating it out in purgatory first. And besides, you're the doctor—I'm sure you can figure out how to defibrillate your own heart."

She leaned against the lip of my windowsill, straining her neck to spy on Remle as well.

"The NBA rejection letter? You do me proud, young Skywalker."

She shrugged and smiled, tucking a strand of sable colored hair behind her ear.

"What do you think she's doing out there?" Meadow craned her neck further, rolling onto her tiptoes.

"Maybe texting a friend about what assholes the people at Lakshmi are."

"Asshole, singular." Meadow held up a finger in my direction. "Considering you aren't even the one to reject them in person, it would be a single asshole."

"Fair point." I laughed. "You are the very best gate keeper."

"She left her oversized gift basket." Meadow followed me out of my office and back to the tasting room. "What should I do with it?"

I could see behind the cellophane and bee-adorned ribbons she'd made a stop at Honey Bunz on her way to visit me. More than likely also stops at the other shops in the area. While it was nice of her to shop locally, I wasn't swayed.

"I'll take it." I told Meadow, wrapping my arm around it, "I need to head up to the airstrip. Gavin texted and told me my bottle samples have arrived."

The basket Remle left behind was practically as wide as my chest. It was also heavy as hell. It appeared she bought out every store on main street. The woman went all out in her attempts to woo me.

"No opening the boxes until you come back here. You promised we could experience opening them *together*."

Meadow shook her pen at me. The stubborn set of her mouth broadcasting she meant serious business.

"Considering you just took Remle to task with a six-year-old letter, I wouldn't dream of disappointing you, madam."

She rolled her eyes, shooing me away.

"Seriously though, I don't tell you thank you enough. I think you should take the rest of the day, grab the corporate card, and go buy yourself something. As a token of my appreciation. We have about a week of calm before the next bottling storm. You deserve it."

"Let's see these beauties!" I rubbed my hands together as Gavin pulled one of my fifteen boxes out of his plane and balanced it on one of his makeshift counters.

"What's so special about these?" Gavin asked as he took a box cutter to the seams.

"They are amber glass." I pulled one from the box, relishing the new design. "It helps prevent light from penetrating through and prematurely aging the bourbon."

I'd spent a small fortune searching the globe for these bottles., My bottle and label artist I'd hired directly from Chennai, and my amber bottles were crafted in the U.K. They looked almost copper in color. Combined with the Sanskrit writing on the bottles and labels, the whole package looked otherworldly.

"I can't wait for the boxes to arrive. Lakshmi's next batch is going to be poetry."

"You know," Gavin took the box and loaded it into the back of my truck, repeating the process with the rest of my order, "I could have sworn it was you who told me years ago this was just a hobby. Something to pass the time. I'm ninety nine percent sure you said you had no interest in doing anything more than 'playing around' with distilling and 'hoping for something neat to pass along to friends.'"

It started that way for sure. When I left Chicago, I just wanted peace and quiet. I had plenty of money from the years of obsessing over my work—so I planned to coast for a while. To see if, after a breather, medicine would appeal to me again. Instead, I found an intense love for the distilling of spirits. It took all the highly specialized knowledge I had in physics, chemistry, biology, and funneled them into something new which challenged me but thrilled me with its rewards at the same time.

"What can I say? I like the company." I tossed a beer toward Gavin.

"You're full of shit." He pointed the neck of the bottle at me. "Me and Meadow are the only people you tolerate. Not like I blame you."

The thing I liked best about Sycamore Mountain was, despite it being a relatively small town, people generally gave you a wide berth. Which was exactly how I preferred to live. Gavin wasn't wrong. I kept my circle small.

"What's the deal with the basket?"

He nodded toward the front seat of my truck, where I'd placed Ms. Clay's disingenuous gift.

"An unwelcome solicitor."

He nodded. I thought it was the end of the discussion, but he continued.

"What are you gonna do with it?"

"I figured I'd swing by the White Oak Inn on my way down the hill and give it to Iris. She always has people coming and going, so maybe she can break it apart and give it to people as they check in."

"I'll take the pastries from Honey Bunz." Gavin pointed to the fancy box placed in the middle of my *gift*. "If you're just giving them away, anyway."

"What's mine is yours." I unfolded myself from the

chair, grabbed it from the passenger seat, and tossed the box of scones in his direction.

"Hey, do me a favor?" He followed me to the truck and held onto the doorjamb as I slipped into the driver's side. "Roger Moore's not feeling so hot and refuses to see the doc. Can you do me a solid and just pop in? Find some excuse? Like, you noticed his horses grazing in your back lot or something?"

If I didn't say yes, I'd be both an asshole to my sole friend in Sycamore Mountain, and heartless to someone who potentially needed medical help.

"Gav—I'm not licensed to practice in North Carolina."

"But you're a doctor who, just with a few questions, can tell Mabel if she has reason to be concerned."

Roger and Mabel Moore were my back acre neighbors. They were one of those generational families who had been in Sycamore Mountain their entire lives. As they progressed in their years, from what I've heard, Roger has become more stubborn in taking trips down the mountain and chalks up most of his ailments to the weather, indigestion, or allergies.

"Fine." I waved him off my door. "I'll stop by after I drop this off."

five
Remle.

That meeting had not gone as expected. Seriously, fuck Shep. I can't believe he let me go in there blind. He had to know about Lakshmi and the shit they pulled on him. I wouldn't want to be part of the Bourbon Association either if I'd received a snotty assed letter in the mail.

After being shamed out of Lakshmi's offices by Jasper's assistant Meadow, I took myself on a driving tour of his property. Beautiful didn't quite reach just how idyllic his property was. He had grain fields, lavender fields, and, of course, a mini forest of white oak trees. Throw in a water mill, some barns and trails, and the guy owned an oil painting made real.

"What's that?" I asked Iris when I finally made it back to the Inn.

Of course, I knew what "that" was given it had been purchased and curated less than four hours ago. On her counter sat my gift basket. Its insides split apart and picked over. The one I'd left for Jasper.

"Oh, Jasper stopped by and left it for me. Said he'd received the basket and had no use for it, and I should leave it here for my customers. Isn't he a sweetheart? So go ahead and take what you want! There are so many great products in here from practically every locally owned store down on Main Street."

She grabbed a box of artisan chocolates I'd purchased at Finley's Market and bit into one. I watched her face relax into an indulgent sigh while she savored the piece in her mouth. I didn't fault her for enjoying my gift. But, what a shitty thing to do. Did Jasper know I was staying here and used this as a double *fuck you*? Like, I get it. The NBA did him dirty, but did he have to be such an asshole about it?

"Did Jasper say anything about why he had this big basket?"

"He said a salesperson had left it for him, and since it was just him and Meadow, the two of them couldn't possibly eat all of this food. He decided to share the love and thought the Inn would be a good place to leave it. You know, with all the vistors coming and going. Plus what a great opportunity for them to learn about the local businesses."

My beautiful basket. At least it was being enjoyed by people who would appreciate it. I guess I could understand Jasper's logic. It still felt like a targeted attack.

"People in this town have a lot of opinions about Mr. Raj. You know, when someone is so private, all the old biddies in this town like to fill the information hole with their own jabber jaws." She laughed, breaking off another piece of chocolate and placing it in her mouth as she continued. "But he's always been kind. My best friend Mabel Moore, she's his neighbor. He always stops by to check in on them. I don't think if he was really as bad as people say he is he would even bother with her and her husband."

I vacillated between wanting to oust him for giving her my basket and using her congenial chatting as a means to get more information on him.

"I must have just missed him," I told Iris. "Meadow told me he was out for the afternoon. I guess if I'd stuck around here and relaxed like you suggested, I could have had a chance to run into him here."

"That's right! I forgot you were going to meet with him!" She actually grabbed at her cheeks, *Home Alone* style, as if me missing my chance to connect with him truly upset her. "Well, maybe you'll have a better chance tomorrow? I wouldn't give up. There aren't many places to hide in a small town. If you aren't able to meet him at his office, more than likely you'll bump into him somewhere in town. And trust me, you won't be able to miss him. He's quite good looking."

She wiped at her brow and fanned herself with a heavy dose of drama.

"I think I'm going to head out and find somewhere for dinner. Any suggestions?"

"Meadow's sister Briar owns the Wallflower Diner down near Finley's. She does comfort foods. Today is hashtag meatloaf Monday."

"Iris, I'm impressed you even know what a hashtag is."

"I have people like Meadow to teach me all about those kinds of things." She winked at me and directed her attention to a family approaching to check out.

"Can I bring you back anything?"

Small towns. I swear within minutes of meeting someone; you felt as if you knew them your entire life.

24

Places like Sycamore Mountain were little hidden diamonds.

"Oh gracious no. I'll be just fine. Besides, I'll see you there shortly. The quilting and knitting club meets at Briar's place at seven o'clock."

Even a side of cheese fries and a stiff drink couldn't gloss over my day. While the diner had charm and everyone was quite pleasant, I had to fight the desire to pay my check and go hide in my hotel room. At the very least, I felt the need to hang out until Iris arrived with the quilting club. She'd been nice enough to suggest somewhere, and mentioned she'd see me so it would be rude to skip out before the aforementioned "seeing" occurred.

Shep: What's the status on Raj?

Whatever sliver of peace I'd found with my carbohydrates and booze disappeared the moment Shep's text dropped in.

Me: Thanks for telling me the NBA gave him the middle finger six years ago.
Me: It wasn't embarrassing at all when his assistant read a rejection letter from NBA word for word while I stood there.

25

Shep: Crap. Did I forget to mention it? Yeah. You know how it is with the "old" guard.

Shep: They had a thing for drawing very strict boundary lines in Bourbon County only.

Shep: But like I said, now is the time for modernization. We aren't just in Kentucky anymore.

Shep: As a salesperson, it's your responsibility to learn how to pivot and sell the new talking points.

Except, I wasn't a salesperson. I was a P.R. gal. I had very little to do with sales. I crafted the message, massaged missteps. I convinced media outlets our stories were newsworthy. It wasn't under my purview to get customers to sign on the dotted line.

Yet, here I was, trying to do that exact thing. It all started with a stupid article in *People* about a famous rapper flying in Lakshmi for his fortieth birthday party. They referred to it as bourbon, which made me wonder if they were members. I brought my concern to Shep and the rest of the board of Bourbon Association and mentioned if Lakshmi was so highly sought after a rapper would pay for it to be flown in; it was definitely a brand that could raise the visibility and caliber of members of the NBA.

Thanks to that single comment, I was the proud owner of a corporate credit card, a travel fund, and a never-ending text stream from Shepard Estes, asking me every second why Lakshmi still wasn't a member.

Me: I'm open to suggestions.

Me: The Lakshmi gatekeeper had zero interest in engaging in any kind of dialogue

Me: Feel free to offer up any thoughts on how to get into his good graces.

Shep: A gift basket works wonders

Me: My gift basket is currently sitting on the check-in counter of the local Inn where Mr. Raj dropped it off. According to the innkeeper he had no interest in receiving gifts from salespeople he wasn't interested in doing business with

That was a stretch. I didn't know for certain that's how he felt. Though it was a sensible assumption.

Shep: Remle, you're the idea woman.

Shep: Your instincts were spot on. We need people like Jasper. How do you tackle public relation problems? Apply that tactic to figuring our Jasper and how to mend that bridge of the old guard.

"Why howdy stranger!" Iris and her crew started to file in, pulling my attention away from Shep and his text messages. "Has Briar been treating you well?"

To be honest, I'd been a little afraid of engaging with Briar. As if Meadow somehow psychically transmitted some kind of message about who I was and what I was in Sycamore Mountain for. I knew, logically, no one would turn down service for something so ridiculous, but I feared stepping foot into Wallflower and having her point to the door and making me leave like a chastised puppy.

Instead, I stayed low key. Smiled and said thank you—not like it was out of the ordinary—and just minded my p's and q's just in case more than three sentences would make Briar wonder who I was and why I was eating cheese fries and drinking a Kaluha milkshake in her establishment.

The group began pushing the two person tables together to form one long banquet style table. While some organized the place settings, others laid out their quilting patterns and various spools of thread for knitting. It looked like they expected about twelve people.

"You know, Iris, I can't wait to tell all of my friends in Lexington about Sycamore Mountain. I had no idea this gorgeous slice of heaven existed not even a half day's drive from me."

"As much as I love our little hidden gem," she leaned in with a conspiratorial gleam in her eyes, "We kind of also need the publicity. Even if the word of mouth is a steady trickle. A town stagnates if new people aren't discovering it."

She was so right. It was then a genius idea struck me. Perhaps it was the assist I needed to get Jasper to at least give me the time of day.

"Did you know that the National Bourbon Association has something called *The Bourbon Trail?*" I asked her, internally jumping in excitement for the glorious opportunity to plant the seed.

"What's the Bourbon Trail?" One of Iris's friends asked.

"It's a map we put out every year which lists all the distilleries who are part of the NBA. It's a neat little booklet that talks about the distillery, the local area around it, tourist information such as places to stay, eat, and shop. We started it a few years ago. I can't tell you how beneficial it's been for our customers to get new people to come and visit. A real boon for their local economies too because, of course, once they've come to visit the distillery, they like to stop for lunch and do a little shopping. Depending on how far away they are from home, more than likely they're at least making a weekend out of it."

I had the entire table held in rapt attention.

"How do you get on that list?" the same friend asked.

"You need to be a member," I said. "I'm actually hoping to get a meeting with Mr. Raj sometime this week. So if you see him, let him know what a great benefit it could be to Sycamore Mountain. I have a few Bourbon Trail books and maps I can leave you all, if you want to check it out?"

I fished the three I carried in my briefcase. I knew I had more back at the hotel. We tended to leave them at hotels in the towns that had bourbon trail distilleries.

"And just think, if Lakshmi were on the list, we could have a cute little set up in Iris's lobby for the maps and promotional materials. You'd also have marketing dollars from NBA to help promote you as a new partner. We could have so much fun putting together some kind of promotion to get people here!"

"Did you hear that, Briar?" Iris called to her from across

the restaurant. "Tell your sister that when Remle comes calling, she should definitely make sure to get her on Jasper's calendar. The town depends on it."

Game, set, match, Mr. Raj.

six

Jasper

" Are you kidding me?"

I heard Meadow all the way in my residence. It wasn't even eight o'clock yet. Meadow liked to get an early start on Tuesdays because she had classes on Tuesday afternoons, but I never realized how easily the sound carried through the distillery and into my private rooms.

Granted, my day typically started around five. She hadn't woken me up or anything, but I had been hyper focused on a project from my bed. I tossed off my covers, threw on a pair of jeans and a T-shirt, and plodded to our reception area.

"What's the matter?"

There was a coffee waiting for me on the counter. On a typical day, I liked to play barista on our JURA espresso machine. But, when she came in early, she tended to swing by Honey Bunz and pick up lattes for both of us. Their honey latte was something I had tried repeatedly to replicate, and it was never quite up to par.

"There are twenty-eight voice mail messages." She handed me the list of the ones she'd taken down already while she continued to listen to them. "Iris has the town all riled up about something called a Bourbon Trail. She says that the town needs you to join the trail for the sake of the local economy."

I took the pile she'd already amassed. What on earth? I'd just seen the woman yesterday afternoon, and she made no mention of this.

"Oh! Mr. Raj, I didn't expect to see you standing here in anticipation of my return!"

Meadow and I had been so wrapped up in sorting through the never-ending voicemails that neither of us had seen, or heard, the charming red head from the day before walking up our driveway.

"I'm Remle Clay. I'm so glad I caught you today. I'm sorry I missed you yesterday."

Her hair was up in a ponytail today. Yesterday's summer kissed dress had been replaced by a pair of black pants highlighting every curve, and a blouse which lovingly cradled the most delectable breasts. If yesterday she'd been a tantalizing summer breeze—today she was August heat in head to toe black with the exception of a pair of red kitten heels.

Why couldn't I stop noticing the smallest details of her outfit? Like the subtle windowpane pattern on her blouse, or the sweet bows on her heels. The eden-esque red hue coloring her lips had all kinds of naughty images dancing through my imagination.

"Mr. Raj?" She smiled, showing off a perfectly aligned set of pearly whites.

Meadow and I locked eyes, and hers broadcast clear discomfort.

"It was so sweet of you to donate the gift basket to the White Oak Inn. All of my fellow travelers certainly appreciated the delectable spread. It's just such a shame you weren't able to enjoy it yourselves. Though I completely understand how difficult it would be to try to consume all of those calories, just between the two of you. That's what I love about small towns." Remle continued, "Everyone looks out for everyone."

I had no idea she'd been staying at the Inn. Of course, why wouldn't she be staying at the Inn? So stupid of me.

"Anyway, I know you are really busy. Meadow has apprised me repeatedly of your jam-packed schedule, so I don't want to take up too much of your time."

She dug around in a messenger bag she had strapped over her shoulder.

"I wanted first to offer my most sincere apology. The letter you received from the National Bourbon Association a few years back is not representative of the new president and his wishes for a more inclusive and broad-based association. There's been a changing of the guard, one could say, a transition of sorts between the older generation who believed Kentucky was the be all and end all for bourbon, and those of us that are a bit more *arms wide open* in our approach. The letter was uncalled for. I would love to make it up to you if you'd give me the opportunity to take you to lunch sometime."

Meadow continued to gawk at me. She pulled a folder from the shelves behind where she sat. The folder was the universal *I'm so busy I need this meeting cut short* folder she'd used to interrupt a conversation.

"Also, I ran into the knitting and quilting club last night while I was having dinner. Such a lovely group of ladies. Anyhow, they were talking about how they wished tourism here was more dependable and less sporadic. I mentioned to them I was meeting with you about potentially joining the Bourbon Association and hopefully, if all went well, they'd soon be added to our Bourbon Trail map."

She handed me a booklet explaining the benefits of membership, as well as the aforementioned trail map.

"Bourbon Trail cities and towns do report as much as a twenty percent uptick in tourism, especially around Bourbon Appreciation Week, which is occurring in..." She glanced at her Apple Watch as if she didn't have the date memorized. I'm sure everyone at that association counted it down like Christmas. "Exactly thirteen days from today. Obviously, you probably wouldn't catch the benefits from this year's bourbon celebration, but next year, certainly."

"Jasper, you have an eight-thirty and we need to go over figures," Meadow cut in, her mouth slowly morphing from a frown to a scowl.

"Thank you, Ms. Clay." I extended my hand. "Lakshmi prides itself on being eclectic. Something exclusive and hard to come by. We aren't for the masses on some hunt for the next bourbon tasting."

"Of course." The smile never left her face. I couldn't stop staring at her. It wasn't even an inauthentic smile. It felt genuine. As if we really were friends and this were a social call. Those big blue eyes of hers were open windows that projected the truth of her smile.

There was something... uncomfortable in feeling her gaze. It was a business transaction. That was it. She wanted me to be part of her association and I said no, or was working my way to saying no. Why, though, did it feel like that smile was something else? Something deeper? We didn't know each other. But it felt strange.

"If you change your mind, I have plenty of ideas on how Lakshmi's exclusive nature could actually blend quite well with being part of our association and with the Bourbon Trail itself." She spun on her pointy heel, waved her classic French manicured fingertips, and skipped out our front door.

"Thanks for the save!" I tapped Meadow's shoulder with the packet of information from Remle.

"You dropped the gift basket she gave you back at the hotel she's staying at? Damn, bro."

"The thought honestly hadn't even crossed my mind. I was with Gav, and he suggested it. In hindsight, it was like a next level asshole kind of move."

"Well. It made a point." Meadow shrugged with a giggle.

Not that it was any of my business how Meadow got so salty. The interaction made me pause. Unfortunately, my mom's number appeared on my cell phone just as I was about to explain to her the difference between declining meetings and humiliating people.

"Mumma, is everything okay?"

"It will be better when you come to your senses and come home back to Chicago. I can talk to your auntie and see if your Uncle Raj can get you a position at his hospital."

It was always the same. While I never expected to be the black sheep of the family, I also didn't expect it would feel so insignificant. I thought if I upset my parents, that burden would weigh on me every day. It doesn't. Even the guilt laden phone calls from Mumma were akin to a fruit fly dipping in and out of my ear.

35

"Mumma, it's only seven-thirty by you. What are you doing up so early making phone calls? Is there something the matter? Is Baba okay?"

"He's fine. He left for golfing with your uncles. I'm calling because I had lunch yesterday with Adithi and Kabita. You know Kabita, her daughter, Gita went to school with you. She's getting married, Gita is. I met Gita's nayan, Mahadeva. I think that we should create bio-data for you. She matched Gita with her fiancé in less than two months. Six months later, now they're getting married. He's from a good family. Professors. So smart. He has a tech firm. Their kids will be so sciency. Gita is a pharmacist, but I know you remember that."

I should have known. The calls about me returning to medicine had waned as the success of Lakshmi rose in prominence. However, as the older of the two siblings, I knew my mother's biological clock was pounding—in relation to *me* getting married and having babies.

I didn't want a matchmaker finding someone for me. It wasn't even about a love marriage versus an arranged marriage. My love right now was Lakshmi. It filled me with so much pride; I didn't have room in my soul for anything else. She was the first thing I thought about in the morning, and the last thing I thought about when I went to bed. I had hopes and dreams for her. Every emotion one would attribute to a spouse—minus the sex, of course—I felt for my business.

"Mumma, no. Call Meera. Have *her* make bio-data. Marry her off. She's the one you brag about, anyway."

I heard her disapproval in a telltale whine in the back of her throat. It was a sound that would make Meera and I scamper back to our bedrooms growing up, knowing we'd pushed too far. Now, though, being a thousand miles away, I knew it was simply time to cut the call short.

"Mumma, I need to go. I have people expecting me in a meeting. My love to you and Baba."

"Bio-data?" Meadow sauntered into my office and took a seat across from my desk.

"My mom wants to hire a matchmaker to find me a wife. They put together bio-data that they swap like poker chips. It's like a bible of who I am, what I do for work, how many siblings I have, what my parents do, where we all went to college. What town in India my parents are from. All of it to pass judgement or assess my value as a potential husband."

"Can I have your space? God, that seems like it would be so much easier than swiping right and left for infinity. Seriously. Call your mom. She can bio-data me to her heart's content."

"Did you need something, Meadow?"

I tried to control my annoyance. It wasn't Meadow who'd set my mood on edge. I just wished for once my parents would find what I did impressive. I wanted them to move past the great disappointment of me abandoning medicine and realize what I did here not only made me happy but was pretty awesome too. How many of her friends can say their kids work with celebrities and rock stars? Not many of them, I'm guessing.

"Not really. You left all the information on the Bourbon Trail on my desk. I didn't know if you intended to leave it so I could throw it away or if you wanted me to file it, or if you wanted it in here."

I didn't either. Know what she should do with it, I meant. I should throw it away and forget all about Ms. Clay. But there was something about her that piqued my curiosity. Her confidence we were a perfect pair had taken up residence in my thoughts.

"Let me look at it." I made a show of sighing dramatically, as if the very task was trying. "I guess I should know why I'm saying no when all twenty-eight residents of Sycamore Mountain roll up with pitchforks because I said no."

A delivery truck rumbled up our driveway, pulling her focus back to the front door. I hoped it was my boxes, as bottling the newest batch began the following week. We'd already sold out. When I started Lakshmi, I never imagined it would become in demand.

I owed a lot of my success to my friend, Gemini. She worked with Chef Tobin Laurent—who was quite possibly one of the most sought-after chefs in the country, and when they started offering Lakshmi bourbon at his establishments, Lakshmi took off. While Tobin leaving for Las Vegas to open a restaurant had been a life-altering event for Gemini, it launched Lakshmi into the stratosphere. Suddenly celebrities were seen with my bourbon bottles in his restaurant and then some of the more exclusive sipping clubs on the strip—and now we'd morphed from a single batch in a year, to biannual batches, and now we would attempt quarterly batching just to keep up with demands.

I was at the point where Lakshmi needed more than just Meadow, me, and a temporary staff. Sooner than I probably realized, I would need a full team. Remle was right about one thing. Lakshmi could be so much bigger. In fact, it was on the precipice of becoming so.

I brought up LinkedIn on my browser and typed in Remle's name. She was the only profile that popped up with such an unusual name. Even her picture took my breath away. I'd seen her in a relaxed sundress, and a professional pantsuit. Her headshots for LinkedIn might have been my favorite by far. She wore a royal blue blouse, her hair all pretty and wavy, holding a gorgeous chestnut colored horse by the bridle. There were so many details about the picture that imprisoned my attention for long minutes. The casual way the breeze flirted with the waves of her hair, pushing it perfectly away from her face. The graceful slope of her neck which the photographer had captured at the perfect moment when she'd been looking at her horse and just happened to look toward the camera. She smiled so wide I could see all the way to her molars, but it didn't read as phony. The smile felt warm, inviting even. Just as she'd been less than an hour ago.

She went to the University of Kentucky—hence the blue blouse. That UK pride ran deep in their veins. My college roommate, despite being at one of the most prestigious colleges in the country, shamelessly sported his UK Wildcats T-shirts every Saturday morning, and all through basketball season. He always said people didn't come to Northwestern for the sports. That was true, at least.

Remle was a member of the Alpha Delta Pi sorority, double majored in Public Relations and Journalism, and graduated Magna Cum Laude. She'd worked for the National Bourbon Association since her graduation in two thousand and nine. Based on the host of compliments, recommendations, and associates singing her praises on the social network—I could surmise not only was she a high-achiever but also ridiculously well liked. Perhaps she wasn't as disingenuous as I'd first assumed.

seven

Remle.

If Jasper wanted to toss aside my gift basket, fine. If he believed he was too good for the NBA, that was okay too. He could believe his own social cred and connection to celebrities would keep him successful and above the water. Maybe it could. I would show him how he could have the best of both worlds: exclusive and accessible.

There were plenty of labels out there doing it, but none did it better than Buffalo Trace. Their Old Rip Van Winkle, Van Winkle Special, Van Winkle Family, and Pappy Van Winkle lines could turn even the most well-heeled gentleman into a black Friday shopper at Walmart. Their labels were separate and distinct, but still under the house of Buffalo Trace. It's what I imagined Lakshmi could become.

When Jasper mentioned they were exclusive, he hadn't been kidding. With the exception of a local bar here in town, a place called the Tuckaway Tavern in hill country, and a few ultra-exclusive resort restaurants, Lakshmi was primarily word of mouth, and only available to people with extra deep pockets. Where a bottle of well-aged Pappy could net upwards of five thousand dollars, Lakshmi's demand was so high, their bottles aftermarket could sell for as much too. Shocking. Pappy had longevity on its side. Pappy's demand came from the age of the spirit, usually between fifteen and twenty-three years. Lakshmi just passed the five-year mark. They didn't have extended period aging yet. I couldn't even imagine what it would net in later years.

"What exactly is it that you're looking for?"

A lovely young man, probably still in high school, directed me to the row of books discussing the basics of spirits at the local book store. I wasn't sure what I was looking for. I knew the basics of the distilling process practically through osmosis, having worked in the industry since college.

"I'll know it when I see it, I guess. I need any book you have on bourbon and whiskey. Whether it's how to make the drinks, the history, anything."

"You probably need to go to Charlotte or Raleigh for that kinda thing. We don't have a lot of inventory. Or maybe online?" He ran his hand along the back of his neck, shrugging as he did so.

"It's fine. Honestly, I'm just browsing. If I find what I'm looking for, great. If not, I'll see what I can find online."

He was right, of course. The bookstore held little I found useful, though the atmosphere was quite cozy with its artsy, coffee shop/bookstore, vibe.

"You've practically grown branches you've been hunched over these books for so long." A man with a tightly trimmed beard and glasses stood at my elbow. Having not seen him approach, his voice startled me back to reality, skyrocketing me quickly from the rabbit hole of research I'd submerged into.

"I didn't mean to startle you." He bit his lip, which suppressed a wide smile from spreading even further. "I'm Ian. This is my little slice of heaven. I thought I'd bring you some water, and see if maybe I could interest you in a coffee or maybe a scone? I get them from my friend over at Honey Bunz."

I gratefully accepted the water and cleared the glass in three not very lady like gulps. Burying oneself in books apparently works up quite the thirst. Ian turned to the self-service station and grabbed the water pitcher, returning to fill up my glass once again.

"What are you reading about? Is there anything I can pull for you?"

"Not really, I don't think. The problem is, I'm not entirely sure what I'm looking for. I'm trying to read up on the distilleries in the area. Whether it's Lakshmi or some of the whiskey distilleries. And not just here in Sycamore Mountain, but in this region in general."

"You must be Remle Clay!" He laughed, taking the seat across from me. "Iris's needle brigade was here earlier today, asking us to sign the petition for Jasper so we can be added to the Bourbon Trail. Whatever it was that you pitched to them last night, it's got them all fired up."

Small towns. Everyone knew your business. Word sure had spread fast. I mean, great for me I guess, if Iris had everyone all riled.

"Good luck with that one." He pointed toward the glass front of his building. I turned to see the man of the hour staring at me from across the street.

"I know. He doesn't talk to anyone. He hates people in

general. No one really knows much about him. I've heard it all."

Ian pulled one of the books I had piled on the side of my table and flipped through it.

"He's actually a really nice guy. He hates being the center of attention. His mentor is a silent partner in this store, so I probably have more insight into Jasper than most. I was the first one to meet him. It may have been me who suggested he purchase the watermill property."

I wanted to ask so many questions. Like why was he practically a digital ghost? What drove him? What were his goals for Lakshmi? What made him tick? Why the cloak and dagger all over town?

"If he's been here for five years, clearly, he intends to stay awhile. So why not, you know, be social? Does he realize he's the town misanthrope?"

Ian waved goodbye to someone leaving the store but remained seated at my table with me.

"Does he actively think about it?" he replied. "Probably not. Though I'm sure he realizes he's a bit of a mystery to most of the people in this town. He kind of engineered it that way. I mean, I thought after a few years the whole burned out super doctor thing would run its course."

He held up his hand as if to say "stop." Though I hadn't even made a gesture that I planned to ask a question. Maybe he was stopping himself from saying too much.

"It's not my place to speculate, obviously. Maybe he's just become so used to operating the way he has he's forgotten what it's like to be social."

Ian pointed across the street to where Jasper stood inside some kind of art studio, having a deep discussion with a woman behind the counter. While inherently I'd noticed his features during our brief interactions, it hadn't quite sunk in how *attractive* he was. In profile, I could see how well he filled his shirt and jeans. Distilling, I'd learned over the years, is quite a workout and it was evident on the very shapely body of Mr. Jasper Raj. At the moment he wore glasses, and I wondered if they were readers or for driving. Either way they were definitely doing something to my libido. I had a thing for intelligence. Give me a man who could wax poetic on the struggle of mankind symbolized in the cockroach in Kafka's *Metamorphosis* and I was jelly. Somehow glasses and tailored clothes on men, for me, always gave off that vibe.

"You said he's a doctor?"

"He's not. Not anymore. He doesn't carry a license to practice anymore. But his mentor, my friend, Dr. Zane, owns a house up in the mountains near where Jasper lives. Jasper came here something like six and a half years ago, needing an escape. I was the one to meet him at Zane's house with the keys. God, he looked absolutely wrecked. Anyway, I don't know what happened. Or why he decided to leave medicine, but from the way Zane sounded when he called me, I've always assumed something bad happened. But again, it's his story to tell, not mine."

eight

Jasper

"We're getting the viewing room ready." The gallery receptionist returned with a mug of coffee.

The paintings I commissioned were finally finished. Meadow and I worked out the exact place to hang each of them within the distillery's tasting spaces. It was going to be magnificent.

It was her hair that caught my eye. That high ponytail of burnished sunset hair, swishing back and forth like a proud show pony. From across the street, I could see her and Ian carrying on quite a genial conversation, which surprised me. First, because Ian tended to keep to himself—sort of like me. Also, Remle had only been in town for a day and a half. Somehow within that span of time, all of Sycamore Mountain had sheltered her under their collective wings.

I didn't blame any of them. While persistent, and definitely more extroverted than made me comfortable, I could see where her bubbliness would be charming to some.

As Ian spoke, she twirled a piece of her hair, almost subconsciously, a soft smile on her lips as they chatted.

I wondered if her hair was as soft as it looked. The unwelcome thought had to be the influence of my mother's phone call. All of this talk about bio-data, matchmakers, and family shame. It wasn't because her charm somehow vexed me in a way I'd never experienced before.

Ian looked up from the table and noticed me staring at them. His momentary pause triggered Remle to look in the same direction. Trapped. That's what she made me feel with those wide, azure-colored eyes. Despite the casual nature of their glances, the curiosity in Remle's gaze felt almost pleasant. Like a passing breeze.

"Mr. Raj? The paintings are hung just over here." The receptionist guided me to a blank wall where my four beauties hung.

The soft sigh of the door opening carried all the way to where I stood. My focus was on the paintings, but on a molecular level, my body knew whose feet stepped over the threshold. I never heard her take a single step in the open, marble space. One moment I stood alone, and the next she stood shoulder to shoulder with me.

"I don't mean to intrude in your showing," her sweet, softly southern voice carried across the space, "I was leaving the bookstore and saw these paintings and my stars. I've never seen anything like these!"

She'd changed her clothes since she'd visited my office. She wore a sweet, embroidered top with little flowers along the collar and a pair of jeans that had me instantly hard. They fit her like a second skin. As if someone made them just for her. The fabric caressed her hips and thighs in such a delectable way it had me thinking dirty thoughts. I wanted to trace my fingers up those thighs, to where they met. I bet she blushed so beautifully in that pale skin.

"No?" Her voice cut into my musings. She'd been speaking to me while I ogled her and thought inappropriate thoughts. I didn't even have a lack of sleep to blame my inability to focus. Next week was when all the physical work at Lakshmi started with bottling and such. Right now, my days pretty much coasted along.

"Can you repeat that? I think I missed what you said."

She grabbed at a necklace resting in the divot of her neck and pulled it around its chain. Up close, I was able to appreciate the constellation of freckles dotting her ivory skin. There was a collection of them running from her collarbone up the side of her neck like a trail of breadcrumbs that begged for my lips and tongue.

"I asked if they were commissions."

"Oh, yes. They were. The gallery owner is friends with an artist by the name of Harsh Malik in Buffalo, New York. I saw a painting of hers of the goddess Lakshmi, and I found it so beautiful it left me speechless. Unfortunately, the painting already had an owner. She has the exact aesthetic I wanted in the distillery. So, she painted these for me."

The colors were so vivid it was impossible not to *feel* each sensual moment in them. I'd asked Harsh to paint me various scenes from the Kama Sutra. I watched Remle examine each of my four commissions. A few times, I noticed she'd reach out to touch the canvases and pull back at the last moment. I felt the same way. I wanted to physically experience the beauty of the paintings against my fingertips, but thinking better of it so as not to ruin the art.

I wanted to explain each of them. To demonstrate how much I'd learned from my intensive studies. To connect the *why's* for her, rather than waiting for her to try to figure it out.

"I grew up Catholic," I told her, by way of explanation. "There is so much about India that is immersed in the Hindu faith, I decided to take classes online."

After I left the hospital, I felt lost. Rudderless but not in a struggling to find the meaning of life kind of way. More in a what do I do with my brain if I'm on permanent vacation mode. Medicine requires you to be firing on all cylinders all the time. When one slams on those career brakes with no alternative, the mind begins to get restless.

"Naturally, over the course of study and discussion of other students of Hinduism, the Kama Sutra is oftentimes brought up since it's so misunderstood. The Kama Sutra is about more than just eroticism, or sex, really. It's about finding and taking pleasure in all aspects of life. Living with passion in everything you do. I think it's quite beautiful. It really resonated with what I'm doing with Lakshmi."

From my vantage point, it appeared Remle lingered over *Padmasana,* which illustrated a woman cradled in her lover's lap, with their legs bent over one another like a lotus flower. It was incredibly intimate. If I had to pick, probably my favorite.

"I really like how Harsh used the gold, copper, and bronze, in that one to highlight where the woman ends, and the man begins, is really a joining. It's incredibly intimate." Her voice was as soft as a sigh. I watched her eyes track up and down the large painting, lingering over where the two lovers were joined. She absorbed the painting in one final look before moving on to the next in the series, *Peasant.* Where *Padmasana* was intimate and sensual, *Peasant* was erotic. It was a picture of a woman cradled between the legs of a seated man, her legs resting on the outsides of his legs while he controlled how wide she was spread for him.

"I can't decide which of them is my favorite. But it's a toss-up between *Padmasana* and *Peasant*. They're like opposite sides of the same coin."

Her focus snapped from taking a lingering journey up and down the next canvas and directly to me. There was heat in her eyes which had nothing to do with anger and everything to do with lust. I could practically taste how erotic she found the painting. Smell the sweet citrus of her perfume as her body temperature raised.

"I'm not tracking," she politely demurred, "one is soft and loving—an expression of the deepest form of intimacy. And the next one is almost vulgar. Carnal. One would say the first is all about making love, and this one." She pointed her lovely, manicured finger at the canvas. "Feels like she's nothing but a whore. He's fucking her. Just flat out."

It charmed me how she blushed. She was southern proper with a capital s and a capital p. She probably presented at Cotillion, had friends named Thaddeus or Thurston, and counted down to the Bluegrass at Keenland like it was Christmas morning.

"Remle." I corralled my entertained delight to just a smile. "Don't you think sharing your basest, most carnal, and perhaps socially inappropriate desires with your sexual partner is the ultimate expression of intimacy? Sure, making love is intense, and sometimes it can feel transcendent. But knowing that you are free to express yourself sexually down whatever road that takes you without fear of judgment? I don't think there is anything more intimate."

The more I talked, the deeper the flush around her chest and neck became. The white shirt she wore only created a spotlight on that flush. I wondered if her skin warmed when she flushed like that. If my lips went to her pulse point, would it be warmer than the rest of her skin? Would her perfume smell stronger? Would her skin feel different with that flush? Being this close to her, while staring at both sensual and overtly sexual paintings, had a slideshow of tawdry images flipping in my mind's eye.

"That flush looks so beautiful on you." I ran a finger down along the bend of her jaw, loving the way she shivered for me.

"Mr. Raj, if these all meet your approval, we can have someone come by tomorrow to install them?"

I'd been so enthralled with our sensual bubble; I'd forgotten entirely we had company.

"Of course. Please coordinate with Meadow for an appropriate delivery time."

The interruption cooled the momentary heat between us. Remle ran her hands down her haunches. Concurrently she shook her head, as if one motion could clear the haze of whatever connection between us I'd just experienced.

"Well, Mr. Raj, thank you for sharing your new artwork with me. I'm sure it will look phenomenal in your distillery."

She extended her hand in my direction. I took it. But instead of shaking it, I simply held it. Her satiny skin felt cool to the touch, despite the heat in her neck. Her French tipped fingers grazed against mine in subtle tickle.

"I can have Meadow call you tomorrow and let you know when they're installed. So you can appreciate them in their intended spaces?"

I'd invited women over to my place before. Many times. Any number of occasions. Some sexual in nature and other times—like this thing with Remle—it was simply a courtesy. Since she was here and liked the paintings. There was absolutely no reason for me to fear her rejection. I needed to get out of the gallery. Whatever had zinged between the two of us while we looked at the artwork was messing with my common sense.

"Give Meadow a call. You know, if you decide, you want to come see the paintings."

My feet couldn't get me out of there fast enough. If it was possible to trip over your words and feet concurrently, I'm certain I was doing it. Remle may or may not have said something as I exited. I was too distracted with getting *out* to pay attention to my surroundings.

nine

Remie.

Those paintings had to be the most erotic things I'd witnessed in person. Books and movies, notwithstanding. It was different though, when a combination of colors swiped across a piece of canvas could evoke such sensuality. I felt the sighs in those paintings, the wet heat of sex, the thick moans of pleasure. Even though we stood still and said nothing at all, each one of them felt both hushed and noisy concurrently. Poetry. That's what they were.

Did I go back to the hotel, search Netflix, and watch *The Kama Sutra* movie? You bet I did. Did I imagine it was Jasper and I enmeshed in a tangle of limbs, panting and moaning out climax after mind altering climax. Also, an affirmative. Was it Jasper I imagined held me open and sensuously explored every inch of body while I took my pleasure into my own hands? A hundred percent. More than once. I may have given myself carpal tunnel.

He'd also given me the tiniest peek into him as a person. I think it got me even more than the paintings had. I liked it.

52

It made me feel—or maybe hope—the inch I'd won might mean he was curious enough to consider my proposal.

The proposal which, as I'd lay in bed reminiscing over the previous evening, expanded into quite possibly the most brilliant idea. It's what had me practically dancing through my shower, make-up, and hair. The idea shimmered in front of me like an unmined diamond with such distraction I paid little attention to the clothes I threw on before practically running to my car.

I'd not connected with Meadow to find out what time the paintings were being delivered. It didn't matter, to be honest. The idea was so grand, even if I missed seeing the paintings when they were installed—if Jasper took the time to hear my idea—it would a hundred percent be worth it.

Meadow looked me up and down the moment I crossed the threshold, picked up the phone, and called Jasper on what I assumed was an office intercom.

"J.R., Ms. Clay has made an appearance again this morning."

"I met your sister the other day," I opened, trying for friendly. "I love her diner. It's got such a great vibe."

"Then you should tell my sister."

Meadow went back to looking at her computer screen, occasionally typing.

"I appreciate that you look out for Mr. Raj. Truly. You do a great job as his confidant. I respect that you keep salespeople like me at an arm's distance. But I'm hoping maybe we can be on the same side. I really think that Sycamore Mountain as a whole could benefit from the visibility my association provides."

Meadow gathered her hair into a bun, never taking her eyes off me.

"Ms. Clay, any benefit your association could provide, lost my support the second your colonizing, antebellum, good old boys' club sent Jasper a *Dear John*. Sorry. You can come in here with your wide-eyed apologies and disingenuous smile, but I call 'em like I see 'em."

"I'm sorry?" I felt my spine stretch that extra inch and a half that my mother says my lazy posture always eats up. "The 'good old boys', as you just called them, don't give a hoot about anything other than their old Kentucky home. I promise you, Lakshmi receiving that letter had to do with distilling outside of Kentucky."

"As if they didn't know, with a name like Lakshmi, that Jasper wasn't from the south." Her eyes rounded, broadcasting a pain I hadn't expected to see. "J.R. is pretty much the only person in Sycamore Mountain who gets me. He's been an amazing mentor to me and quite frankly, I will do everything in my power to make sure he isn't hurt, taken advantage of, or embarrassed. I think the old farts who got greedy during Kentucky distilling's heyday realized, *oh shit,* people outside of this state have learned a thing or two! They realize that a tiny, independent distiller like Jasper can run circles around most of your mid-tier distillers last year at half their size, and now they just want him for his money. So they'll fake smile, play nice, deal with the fact he's neither southern nor from Kentucky, because they know he'll bring cash back in."

I hadn't expected the accusation, but I wasn't surprised. However, our new president and board had worked really hard since their installation to move the association into the new millennium. They recognized people from all walks of life, backgrounds, races, and genders were making names for bourbon in big ways. While I'd only been working for the association since I graduated—I could see a significant shift in the industry in those years and it was something I was really proud to be a part of.

"Meadow, please pull up our website and click on the industry tab. We have women distillers, we have men distillers, there are non-binary distillers, and distillers from every background and nationality. Some of those distillers are legacy distillers—meaning they produce over a hundred thousand barrels a year and have been distilling for over a hundred years. I promise. I swear on the Clay name—and in Kentucky family names are the second most respected thing next to God himself—that the only reason Lakshmi's application was denied was because he distills in North Carolina."

I saw our website in the reflection of her glasses while she scrolled. She exited out, seemingly satisfied, and turned to answer the ringing phone. I dared a few steps journey to their gathering room, which housed pictures of their first five years in business. There was a picture of Jasper and an older man. I can only assume it was Dr. Zane, the man Ian told me about, standing at the front doors. Despite the smile on Jasper's face in the picture, he looked gaunt. Easily fifty pounds lighter, heavy bags under his eyes, and no life in them. To be honest, he looked like a living zombie. A complete divergence from the fit, relaxed man who walked toward me with his sleeves rolled up to his elbows. I don't think I'd ever noticed forearms on a man before, but his were shapely and well defined.

"Are those from lifting bourbon barrels?" I nodded at his forearms, my libido apparently deciding to take a swing at making conversation.

Jasper stopped in his tracks and examined his arms.

What a lovely pair of arms they were. The muscles were so well defined; they shifted and bunched with each turn of his palms. He turned them again, so his palms faced up and then turned them palms down once again, laughing.

"I guess they are. I never really paid attention before."

Two awkward people. That's what we suddenly became. Randomly standing in the middle of his gathering room, staring at one another.

"J.R., Gemini is on the phone. She said your cell phone keeps going to voice mail. I'm transferring her to the tasting room phone."

Jasper held up his finger and strode to the ringing phone in the area just to our left. It gave me the opportunity to take in more of Lakshmi with its dark wood, river stone, and greenery. The whole space felt natural and organic, but very much a nod to his Eurasian roots. The chairs surrounding the oversized spotted elm table appeared to have been created from Saris in muted greens and blues. The tile lining the fireplace was a tight paisley pattern reflecting the same styling as the Saris. Over the fireplace was a large, recessed shelf, which held a bronze sculpture of Lakshmi herself posed on a Lotus blossom. The entire space was an art piece.

"I don't know Gem... things are crazy right now." Jasper stood at the bank of windows overlooking that white oak forest synonymous with Sycamore Mountain. I could clearly hear his conversation from where I stood.

"I have barrels that need bottling Saturday. I have a whole crew of people coming in."

I assumed, based on his comment he still contracted his work out. Understandable since he was a boutique distiller, but it also meant he did all the distilling himself. Which was surprising, to say the least.

"Fine. Let me see what I can do. I'll call you back."

By the time I heard his last comment, I had already made my way back to where Meadow sat.

"The art installers aren't coming until later this afternoon," Jasper said, as he hung up the phone. "Probably not until around three."

"Oh, yeah. Of course. The art installers... because I wanted to come and see them hanging in the space. Right."

Now that I stood in Lakshmi, I felt totally stupid for infringing on their space with half-cocked ideas. This morning, it seemed like a brilliant idea. Now? Not so much.

"So..." I played with the tie on my wrap dress, suddenly unsure of my super fantastic plan. "I actually have been thinking a lot about what you said. About how you want to remain an elusive, and very high-end label. I did some research and reflected on some of my larger legacy members like Buffalo Trace and I'm pretty confident my idea is something you'll not only want to hear but will want to implement."

Jasper cocked his head in my direction. It was the first time he looked approachable. The muscles around his eyes had loosened, making him look more friendly and less severe.

"How long are you in town, Ms. Clay?"

"Remle." I tried to suppress the smile that broke across my mouth. "And I'm here until I convince you to join the Bourbon Association."

I winked at him, and he rolled his eyes in return. The motion of rolling his eyes skyward, triggered the muscles in his face to snap back into an emotionless mask. Though, I did witness a wobble in the set of his mouth. Like he wanted to smile but needed to appear businesslike. I saw it, the slow chipping away of the ice around Mr. Misanthrope.

"Or until Friday." I shrugged.

"My friend in Barren Hill needs me to consult on a project. It's about a four-hour drive if you're interested in coming with me. You can tell me all about whatever is in the packet I haven't read yet—and this fantastic new idea—on our way there. Interested?"

"Oh, I don't know..." Four hours in a car with Jasper? I barely knew him. It would be weird Four hours of stunted, but polite conversation to pass the time?

"You seem like an idea person," Jasper pressed, "and the town here seems to be totally enthralled by your charming personality and stunning smile—I think you might be the perfect addition to my friend's project. She needs someone like you—who just digs a new path around a roadblock."

He thought I was stunning? Okay, a stunning smile—but still. Flattery definitely gets one places. Calling me charming and stunning while also complimenting my skills as a P.R. person? Sign me up for whatever you're asking of me.

"How long will we be gone?"

"I'm hoping to make this a day trip. But potentially overnight. We'd be back tomorrow evening at the latest."

Perhaps if we ended up staying the night somewhere, it would only have one bed, and we'd be forced to share. Scratch that, I brought literally nothing appealing in terms of sleepwear on this trip. I had misshapen pajama bottoms the elastic had worn out of, giving me diaper ass, and a ratty old UK T-shirt that was so threadbare my nipples practically poked through the cotton.

"Sure. Why not?"

He actually looked excited. He beamed a smile at me. Not a smirk. Not a halfhearted one corner of his mouth lift— but an actual smile.

"I'll pick you up at the Inn in, let's say, forty-five minutes. Pack a bag just in case. Jeans, T-shirt, gym shoes."

"Gym shoes? Clearly, you're not from the south."

"Chicago." He ran his hand down his mouth, his fingers tracing the smile on his lips.

"Ah, that explains it. All right I'll see you in forty-five."

What on earth was I doing taking a road trip with a near stranger? And why was I over the moon excited about said trip? I needed to get my head examined.

ten

Jasper

"What on earth is all of *that*?"

We hadn't even made it out of the city limits yet. I stopped to top off my gas after picking Remle up from the Inn. She'd said she wanted to grab a few things from the gas station—but a few things apparently were the entire snack aisle.

"I'm pretty sure the rules of a good road trip state regardless of time or distance, if you are driving with friends for an extended amount of time, you must grab all the things from the gas station like you're a kid with a twenty-dollar bill and no supervision."

She proudly displayed the chips, Twizzlers, water bottles, Red Bull, and Reese's Pieces she purchased.

"Do you have any idea what food like this does to your insides?"

"Count on Doctor Raj to come swinging with the Debbie Downer health facts."

Every molecule of my insides which had been feeling

pretty relaxed hardened in the frozen tundra of flashbacks to my past life.

"Wow, in a matter of three days, you've done your due diligence on ferreting out all the details about me. Interesting sales tactic."

I watched her face go from beaming with excitement to chastened in a millisecond. Shit. While I didn't mean to make her feel uncomfortable, she had no right digging into my past. It was mine to tell her. Something I planned on touching on in the simplest terms when we arrived in Barren Hill.

"It wasn't a sales tactic," she replied, wrapping her arms around herself. "People in this town are super chatty. A few of them have mentioned you used to be a doctor, that's all."

"Which is neither up for discussion nor examination."

I felt exposed. Seen in a way which made my skin crawl and sent panic exploding through my nervous system. The people of Sycamore Mountain knew nothing about how I'd come by their tiny town. Hundreds of thousands of dollars had scrubbed my past life from the search engines, guaranteeing no one would find out.

She didn't respond. Instead, she turned toward the window and watched the landscape change. It worked just fine for me, too. The last thing I needed was to engage in a dialogue with someone I barely knew, recounting the worst days of my life.

"Hi, Mom!" Her phone rang sometime later, her bright, cheery voice startling me out of my ruminations.

I'd been deep in reminiscences about my past life. Visiting could have and should have's I thought were long forgotten. So many years of therapy to figure myself out, and with one unexpected comment, I felt unhinged again.

"No, I'm actually in North Carolina for the week."

She continued, trying to talk softer, glancing at me to see if she'd disturbed me.

"Work. Always work."

I liked her laugh. It felt like a cool breeze in the middle of a heat wave. Just a quick second of delicious relief before the summer sun started to sizzle once again. I took my eyes off the road for the briefest of seconds to chance a glance in her direction. She leaned on her palm against the window, drumming her fingers against her cheek.

"I should be back in Lexington sometime on Friday night."

I couldn't make out what her mom said, but whatever it was, caused her to roll her eyes in what clearly was a universal child parent dynamic.

"Mom, I'm thirty-five. I'm perfectly happy with where I am in my life right now."

She had me hanging on her every word. While I wasn't usually one to eavesdrop, something about how similar her conversations were to the ones I had with my mom made me feel a strange kinship with her. Also, it didn't go unnoticed she was older than I thought she was, and much closer to my own forty-one than originally anticipated.

"Look, I've gotta go. I'm driving and I need to focus on where I'm going. Tell Georgina I'm so sad I missed her, and hope Nanny and Pop Pop bring her by later in the summer too."

She disconnected and tossed her phone into the truck's cup holder.

"Let me guess, 'You aren't getting any younger. Don't you realize all the good people are already married and having kids? If you don't pick someone soon, you'll only have the castoffs left to choose from?'"

"Something like that." She giggled. "I swear when I was in college it was nothing but 'don't you even think about getting married to your college boyfriend. There's a whole world of men out there. Go and experience life. Grab that career. Do all the things!' and now she's like 'If you don't get married soon, your eggs are going to rot. I'm gonna die with just Georgina as my grandbaby. Why can't I be like the rest of my friends and have lots of grandbabies to spoil?' I swear every day their interest in my work decreases exponentially in relation to whether or not I have any prospects in the potential husband column."

An image of her pregnant, lazing in the lavender fields by the water mill smashed into my consciousness. Given I knew shit all about her, the picture shocked me more than anything. I needed to figure out a way to get my mother's nagging out of my head. Our conversation was starting to mess with me. As if Remle would even be interested in someone like me.

"So, you had an idea you were going to share with me about Lakshmi?"

I'd discuss anything to get the vision of a pregnant Remle out of my brain. What better way to exorcise it than talking about my one true love? Lakshmi had been born out of a need to find a new purpose. It provided me the greatest solace, and the amount of pride I have for my *little business that could* felt better than every medical accolade I ever received.

"Ohmigosh! Yes I do. Thank you for reminding me."

She wrapped her hands around my bicep, all endearing smile and glistening excitement in her eyes. Her touch created a butterfly effect of sensation through my entire nervous system. One I discovered I not only didn't mind but wanted to feel again.

"You know Buffalo Trace, right?"

Nearly everyone knew the brand. They were one of the biggest distilleries and probably the oldest. The term cornered the market probably was invented in relation to them.

"Of course."

"So, what if you approached your distilling sort of like they do? You have Lakshmi—your standard, high end, exclusive label which continues to operate just as it does today. But you break out and market to the late generation millennials and Gen Z with affordable, accessible—but still super trendy and hip, specialty labels. With these attainable but still exclusive bottles, you can drop down into the one year distilled spirts. Quicker turnaround time. More freedom to experiment." She balanced both of her hands as if weighing each option. "And you base them off the Kama Sutra. Those paintings are... enough to make you flush."

She cleared her throat and shifted in her seat. I wondered if in fact *both* of us felt that odd zing. My conscious took the opportunity to replay once again all the tawdry images I'd had over her in various Kama Sutra poses. And not just a quick blip of a replay, but long, drawn-out images, her back to my front, straddled, spread wide open, her voice keening as I took her over for the third time exploring each erogenous zone. Feeling the lush press of her curves against my groin, the softness between my arms, smelling the tantalizing fresh scent of her perfume while her riot of hair tickled against my cheek.

Shit. The thoughts made me throb with want.

Something I prayed wasn't apparent beneath the driving shaft of my truck.

"Sex sells, right? So why not make something just for the younger generations along the lines of *this isn't your pappi's sipping bourbon?*"

"It might work." I could hear in my voice how affected it sounded. I prayed she didn't notice. Hopefully I passed it off as excited interest. Or at least, moderate interest.

I turned to look at her and watched the relief pour across her features as I did. Was I really that intimidating? I didn't think I was. She demurred with pinkened cheeks.

"That's an impressive amount of thought you put into this." I continued, "Especially considering the risk I could take your idea and never sign with the Bourbon Association."

"It's a risk, sure. But don't all the best things come with a bit of a risk and a leap of faith?"

It was as if she'd been reading my mind earlier. Lakshmi was the biggest risk I'd ever taken. My largest jump. Something in her voice, in the assured way she downloaded her idea, reminded me a lot of me. I could see the same fire in her I felt when making decisions for Lakshmi.

I didn't want to go too deep into it. But Gemini was a renowned chef. Her palate was impeccable. The reason I agreed to come up and help her with this free clinic was so I could get her opinion on some new batch flavors I'd been considering. Those flavors might be good to experiment with "toss away" one-year barrels before committing to longer aging processes.

"Wow. The resort is..."

Our discussion about bourbon and secondary labels got cut short. We made excellent time up to Barren Hill and the

Echo Creek Resort. Gemini requested we meet her at the Tavern off the access road first.

"It's pretty grand. I just want to forewarn you because sometimes it can be a little shocking for some people... Gemini runs the Tuckaway Tavern with her fiancé Finn and his best friend Emmett. Emmett helps Gemini run the kitchen. Finn takes care of the business end of things and the front of the house."

"I'm sure those introductions are probably going to be made inside." She took hold of the door handle and tossed a smile at me.

"Emmett only has one arm," I blurted out, unable to find a more subtle way to discuss the subject quickly. "The last time I came down here, I brought Harmony with me so she could show them all her app, Whiskey Click. Let's just say neither of us was prepared and I think we both made Emmett feel really uncomfortable, unintentionally. I just want to give you the head's up. Before we go in there. His entire left arm was severed in a rail car accident."

"That must make it so hard for him. And you said he's a cook? I can't even imagine having to relearn all those complicated things with only one arm."

I knew very little about Emmett. We'd only had that singular interaction. Other than communicating to Gemini how sorry I was, we'd never spoken about it. I did know, however, Gemini thought very highly of him, and regarded him as the brother she'd never had.

"You're here!" Gemini burst through the door of the Tuckaway Tavern, sprinting toward our truck. With one hearty yank, she had the door open and practically hauled me from the cab before suffocating me in a hug. "I can't thank you enough, Jasper. I owe you, big time. I couldn't think of anyone else who would do this project justice. It's a passion project, for sure."

Remle slid out of my truck from the other side and extended her hand in introduction.

"Hi, Remle. I hope you don't mind me tagging along."

"Any friend of Jasper is a friend of mine!" Gemini clotheslined her with a side hug and led her toward the door of the tavern. "I didn't know you were bringing someone, Jasper. But it's the first week of summer break and the resort is packed to the gills."

"We're sharing a room?" Remle's panicked eyes and perfectly shaped "o" on her bow-shaped lips nearly drew a laugh from me. "Are there two beds?"

"Yes, there are definitely two beds. Cross my heart."

"Guys! We have reinforcements!" Gemini shouted as we crossed the threshold into her restaurant.

"You know Finn and Emmett already." Gemini pointed to Finn, who approached from the bar with a towel slung over his shoulder, and Emmett who pushed through the swinging doors from the kitchen. "This is Emmett's girlfriend, Amelia. My friend Penn—who also happens to own the resort—and his brother Bryce."

Remle and I exchanged greetings with everyone, accepting some water from Finn in the process.

"You haven't yet met Sawyer—who grew up with Penn and Bryce. He's up at the site supervising some of the software installations. And fun fact—Penn is now officially a Chicagoan. He and his soon-to-be wife moved there in January."

"Are you in Chicago too?" Penn held out his hand in a fist pound, seemingly excited to have a friend in his new city.

"Born and raised, visit frequently, but live in North Carolina."

"Jasper owns Lakshmi Bourbon—or is it Lakshmi Whiskey? It's confusing because it's bourbon based on proof and contents, but the box says Whiskey." Gemini asked, looking between me and Penn.

"It's whiskey," I told Gemini, at the same time Remle announced, "It's bourbon."

"According to industry standards," Remle continued, smiling, and winking at me as she did, "Lakshmi is a bourbon. There was some confusion a few years back regarding distilling location, but that has been rectified and hopefully Lakshmi soon will be changing their packaging to acknowledge they are, in fact, the best sipping spirit this side of the Mason-Dixon line!"

"She'd know." I shrugged. "She's from the Bourbon Association."

"Gem... since it's already lunchtime, maybe we can chat on our way up to the site. Especially if Jasper is only here for the day." Finn pulled Gemini to his side, grazing his lips against her hair. The way she leaned into him and sighed. Shit. I wanted that. I wanted to feel comforted by someone else's presence the way she did.

"You're staying the night, aren't you?" Gemini looked at me and then to Remle with pleading eyes. "Penn has Chef Le'Sant cooking for all of us tonight and I really want to catch up with you and learn all about our new friend, Remle."

"I don't have anything packed for a fancy dinner," Remle whispered, arm around my bicep. "You told me grungy clothes like jeans and sneakers. That's all I brought."

"There's a shop up at the resort," Amelia offered. "It's

not huge by any means but they have a lot of sundresses and the like."

Her eyes widened, the color shifting from azure to ocean. "I'll buy it for you," I assured her. "You're my guest. It's the least I could do."

She didn't reply, but we both were gathered into the bustle of the group and funneled into Finn's truck to head out to the site where they collectively had been building a health clinic.

"I know. We're a little crazy." Gemini spun around, hands braced on the headrest of her seat while she spoke to Remle and I in the back seat. "You'd think between the tavern, building a house for the two of us, Emmett renovating *his* house so it is accessible for both him and Amelia *plus* our Veteran's group, we'd have our hands full. But Jasper, you just wouldn't believe how desperately we need a clinic here. Especially up in hill country. Do you know what the mortality rate is for women in labor up in hill country? Sixteen per one hundred thousand. Sixteen! We're above the national mortality rate, Jasper. We needed to do something. It was already a travesty that there was no veteran care. An even larger travesty that injured vets have to travel upward of three hours to get to the nearest VA hospital. The closest regular hospital is over an hour away. I'm hoping this clinic will at least be able to bridge the deficit in care, even if it's a marginal difference."

"I'm happy to help advise you on what is needed and the types of clinicians you should be searching for."

"Well—so here's the stitch. I appreciate anything you can give us. Guidance. Funding. Advice. But I'm hoping, given that you're so close, that um—maybe you'd be willing to come do some volunteering a few days a month?"

Gemini bit her lip and winced. We'd been friends for as long as Lakshmi had been in business. Chef Laurent's restaurant—where Gemini had been Chef de Cuisine—was one of the first to promote the Lakshmi brand. I owed her for that. For my success. For the exposure to people with expensive taste and deep pockets. However, that kind of favor is repaid in—I don't know—free bottles for life. Coming and doing meet and greets, sending signed bottles for her to use promotionally. That kind of debt did not transfer to digging up a buried past and forcing me back into the throes of it.

"Gemini..." I felt the panic in my voice. I knew the tightly wound spool of feelings I held in check was about to not just unravel, but explode into a confetti of loose bits of string. "This goes beyond the pale."

As if she could sense my unease, Remle reached out and snaked her fingers between mine. When I tried to pull away, she only held on tighter. When I looked at her, I saw compassion and understanding in her eyes. It didn't bother me. In fact, it felt oddly grounding.

"Is there a way that he could consult without needing to practice?" Remle asked. "He isn't licensed here. He can't practice."

"Technically, you can," she responded, looking at me, "You did a stint with Doctors Without Borders for a year. You told me the last time you were here—when we were discussing Amelia's, um, injuries."

Amelia and Emmett drove in a separate car, but it was a sensitive subject. Emmett's girlfriend suffered a total femoral amputation as a result of driving over an IED in Afghanistan. If it hadn't been for her Sergeant being quick thinking enough to have her airlifted out of her base, she would have bled out. Losing her leg had to have been severely traumatic, but thanks to that split decision, she had the best surgeons attending to her and taking care of amputation within the safe confines of a hospital. That decision allowed her to live as normal of a life as she could have given the circumstances.

"You are licensed as a humanitarian doctor. This work falls under the umbrella of humanitarian medicine, so you don't need to be licensed here."

I didn't have the strength to answer. Too many things converged at once. That night in December. A terrible blizzard and then a dip into subzero temperatures had left most of Chicago stranded. For me and my team, it meant we were on the floor for going on thirty-six hours trying to grab sleep and food in the brief lulls of activity. And then all hell broke loose. Massive pileup on the highway, fatalities left and right. *I saw her Dr. Raj. Her fingers were moving!*

Even shaking my head repeatedly wouldn't exorcise the demons from inside my thoughts.

"Names are really big things in southern families," Remle whispered, squeezing my hand. "When new kids are born, you get the grandparent's names. Especially on the land-owning side, which in my parent's case was the Clay family. My grandpa Holt—my brother, as firstborn —got his name. Holt Shackleton Clay. My mom's dad though? His name was Elmer. And when I was born, my mom was like, how the hell do we make Elmer sound cute? There's no way my sweet-faced baby girl is going to be saddled with a name like Elmer. Rather than struggle to find a cute way to make Elmer sound feminine, she decided to just flip it backward and name me Remle. I'm pretty sure I'm probably the only Remle in existence. Well, maybe not in existence, but I can never find those cute touristy, miniature license plates with my name on it in gas stations, that's for sure."

The hushed whisper of her voice buffed over some of my most jagged pieces.

"Thank you."

I didn't really know what else to say.

"Why did you tell me that story?"

"Because sometimes it takes looking at something at a different angle for it to not seem so terrible."

eleven

Remle.

J asper was direct. He had an unfiltered personality
which could be occasionally kind of biting and, well,
dickish. However, he was also, without a doubt, the
softest and most sensual kisser. Talk about a
dichotomy. One minute he seemed to be folded into himself,
lost in the recesses of his mind, and the next he had my jaw
cradled in his hand and gently traversed every centimeter of
my upper and lower lips.

"What was that for?"

I couldn't control the smile that broke loose. There had
been this strange undercurrent between Jasper and me since
the gallery. I knew he looked at me as an inconvenience. But
something shifted. Suddenly, I was more. First, it morphed
away from the annoying salesperson to a casual
conversationalist. Then I'm his company on a four-hour
road trip. Now? I was the someone who soothed, and also
who he kissed, apparently. A kiss which was far too intimate
for a person he couldn't stand.

"I was looking at something from a different angle. Someone wise once said it. Confucius maybe."

Gone was the flat line of his lips. Replaced with an honest to goodness smile. A genuine one which caused his eyes to crinkle, and the smallest divot in his cheek to appear.

Where did the kiss leave me? Or us, I guess. If there was an us. Maybe the kiss was a onetime thing. I still needed to return to Lexington and deliver to Shep's obsessively manicured hand, a signed contract. A signed contract from someone I spent the night fantasizing about and now kissing.

"This place is incredible! When do you expect to be open for business?" I asked Gemini.

Gemini, Finn, Emmett, and Jasper had gone into the near-complete office portion of the clinic to discuss what else needed to be done in order to be licensed to practice. It was more than evident the clinic was a labor of love for the entire friend group. Penn and Bryce secured financing. Bryce's girlfriend—an architect—drafted the designs and, from what they told me, found quite a few builders, engineers, and tradesman throughout the area willing to work pro-bono. Amelia connected with the Veteran's Administration to secure jobs for veterans. Where they had gaps in manpower, the whole crew would plan days, weekends, or longer stints such as this one to help the project cross the finish line.

"Hopefully this week." She pulled a water bottle from

the cooler and cleared it in a few sips. "It's why I needed Jasper up here ASAP. He knows way more about staffing a free clinic than I do."

"I swear the woman can't sit still." Her fiancé, Finn, took a seat next to her at the picnic bench we sat on. "First it was renovating the bar, then it was the amputee support group, now she's juggling the free clinic."

There wasn't any bite to his comments. In fact, he smiled down at her while caressing her face. The two of them seemingly transported to an alternate reality where only the two of them existed.

"I think we have everything that we need." Sawyer shuffled from the building, Jasper and Emmett close behind. "All of your networks and systems are triple encrypted. Not only are you HIPPA compliant with these networks, but the network up here is probably more secure than this fancy fucker has at his hotels."

Sawyer arched an eyebrow and cocked his head toward Penn. He and Bryce arrived from around the side of the building where they'd been installing the "Free Clinic" light up sign. By the looks of it, they were only a few touches away from being ready to open.

"Jasper, how soon do you think you can have those resumes looked at?"

He appeared to be lost in thought. There was a pile of papers between his hands. His head was in fact downturn in such a way it would imply he was reading whatever was between his hands. But, even with a second attempt to get his attention, Gemini was unsuccessful in engaging him further into conversation.

"Hey, Penn," Gemini shifted focus, apparently taking note of Jasper's distance, "Jasper's girlfriend here needs a dress for the evening. Can I send the two of them to the resort shop and have her credit it out?"

"I can take care of it," Jasper answered at the same time. I clarified I was not, in fact, his girlfriend.

They all looked at me like I had three heads. They said nothing. Total uncomfortable silence where they all shared knowing looks with one another. I didn't know what to say. I was brought because of my PR acumen. Maybe I should tell them while Jasper and I just lip locked in the car with Gemini on the way up to the clinic, it was literally the first time we'd ever done it. And I still wondered myself if it was a one and done. Instead, I did what all good P.R. people do. I pivoted.

"What time did you say our reservations were?"

"Seven," Penn responded. "It will be nice for our James Beard Award nominated chef," he squeezed Gemini's shoulder and smiled, "to enjoy herself for the night and not have to cook."

"It also doesn't hurt Duane will have to spend the whole night hearing everyone gush about her nomination, either." Emmett snickered, ducking the water bottle Finn chucked in his direction.

"All right, I'm going to take Remle to the hotel giftshop." Gemini pushed herself off the picnic table and swatted at the dust on her jeans. "Men—do whatever manly things you still need to do and I'll see you all at the Cliff at Echo Creek at seven on the button. Jasper, are you coming with us?"

"What about this one?" Gemini held up a jersey knit sundress.

I shook my head, too embarrassed to say why I didn't think it wouldn't work.

"I can't believe the clothes here only go up to a size fourteen. It's ridiculous. Half this shit I couldn't wear, and I'm best friends with the owner!" Gemini continued to flip through rack after rack, trying to find something.

"What about this one?" She pulled out another cotton shift dress. It looked less sausage casing than the last one she'd pulled out, so I took it to go try on.

"I'm not sure how much you know about Jasper's past," I tried to sound like I had any clue, "but did you see how panicked he looked earlier when you asked about volunteering?"

"He told *you* about what happened? Wow."

He hadn't, actually. Not to any huge extent. I could put together the puzzle pieces, and assume something bad must have happened, but I still didn't have any substantive information.

"I don't even have all the details. I just know he was a super important doctor, all the awards and accolades. Then someone died and suddenly the entire medical community treated him like he was a pariah."

"Oh, wow." I peeked around the dressing room curtain. "I knew someone died, but I didn't know about all that other stuff."

I didn't *actually* know someone died. I surmised something bad happened and wondered if it was a dead patient. Mainly because I couldn't imagine what else could possibly be so bad that anytime someone even breathed the suggestion of medicine, he turned into a tightly wound viper.

"Did that one work any better?"

It looked awful. Tight in all the places I really wanted to hide. Like the jelly roll of my midsection.

"You know what? It's fine. I can just hang out in the room. I barely know any of y'all anyway. So maybe this is a sign I should just focus on work and spend the evening working on my status reports for my boss."

"Nonsense!" She yanked open the curtain, speaking face to face. "You came all this way and you're my guest. I'm going to go home and grab a few things from my own closet. We're nearly the same size. I know I have a few eighteens left from the divorce year. What room did they book you in? I'll just come straight up and hand off what I've got."

twelve

Jasper

I felt on edge, and I hated it. This creeping sensation like nothing was right in the world. No matter what you did or who you tried to become, the past always hung out in the shadows to haunt and torture you. Gemini meant well. We'd been friends for a number of years now, and I knew she had no idea of how terrible it was—just getting through each day—trying to forget the worst day and the most terrible mistakes of my life. I still needed therapy each week to work through it.

Forgiveness is hard. Especially forgiving yourself. I'd upgraded from three times a week, to twice a week—and just within the last six months, my therapist said he liked the progression of my journey and now we only met on Fridays. I could survive twenty-four more hours. The flashbacks this time threw me for a loop. They hadn't been so vivid in at least two years. What kind of progress was I really making if, in one fell swoop, a favor from Gemini could send me reeling?

I barely registered Remle's return from downstairs. I

know she wouldn't be happy having to share a room, even if there were two beds. I hoped she didn't think I planned it. Honestly, I tried calling down to reception to get it changed, and they were at full capacity. Even the suites, they told me, were booked. I was certain Penn, Bryce, and Sawyer were using them.

"How are you feeling?" she asked, taking a seat at the end of my bed, resting her hand on my leg.

I hated the question. Hated she'd seen straight into the heart of me. Somehow she guessed at the wound I carried.

"My brother died," she told me. "Just after I graduated from college. He was three years older than me, but without a doubt my best friend. He'd gone snowmobiling in Paoli Peaks with our friends one weekend. It was the winter just after I started at NBA, so I didn't have enough vacation time built up to go for the weekend with them to the cabin. We've gone a million times since we were kids.

"He was always kind of a showboat. He'd do crazy things to get a reaction out of people. He used to drive my mom crazy with high jumps off the cliffs at Three Sisters or riding our uncle's horses with no hands on the reins—just dumb thrill seeker stuff."

The hitch of her breath drew my eyes to hers. There was a sad smile on her face. Those crystalline blue eyes, usually so bright and captivating, had dimmed in their hue.

"His friends told us nothing was out of the ordinary. They assured us he hadn't been doing anything crazy. It was first thing in the morning, right after breakfast, so alcohol wasn't involved—and thankfully, none of those assholes were dumb enough to drink, then take the snowmobiles out. He just took a turn too hard. The snowpack had turned icy overnight, and the vehicle flipped and skid, smashing him into a tree.

"I wasn't even there, but in my mind's eye I still see it. I can imagine what it looked like. We've spent so many winters up there I know what he saw just before he died, because we'd all taken that path so many times."

Her hand rested on my calf. Her nails contracted and relaxed as she told her story, broadcasting her own discomfort. In that slight scratch, I witnessed a similarity to the churning storm inside my own mind.

"It was the worst day of my life. Holt was my best friend. He was always the one I'd call when my mom drove me crazy. He was my sounding board when guys weren't treating me right. He was my everything. And I thought I lost him completely.

"But sometimes you get something great out of your worst tragedies. His girlfriend Mae had been with him. We found out a few months after Holt died Mae was pregnant with Georgina. So, even though we lost Holt—we still have a little piece of him. Sometimes the best things are born out of tragedy. Like Georgina.

"Or I think, in your case, Lakshmi. I don't know your story," she continued, turning to look toward me with tears glistening in her eyes, "but I can guess based on your reactions today, whatever happened, it's pretty bad. And if you don't want to share, I completely understand. But know I'm here. It helps to talk about it. The guilt. The sense of helplessness. The *what ifs* and all the questions that exist in the black hole of loss."

I'd done plenty of talking. Five years' worth of therapy talking. My mind set off alarm bells, telling me to shut this whole thing down. It felt too close. Too *intimate*. But something else craved it. The feeling of closeness with someone who *got it*. I opened my mouth, not entirely sure what would come out—be it a rebuttal or unburdening.

"There was a bad snowstorm in Chicago. Funny," I chuckled at the sad irony, "both of our worst days happened in the winter."

The words shut down the memories in my head. My whole conscious went black momentarily. It felt oddly peaceful, existing in the nothingness.

"I used to be an E.R. trauma surgeon. I worked hard to get to where I had been. Spent years working endless hours —pushing myself to extremes to earn that achievement. I was well-respected. People looked to me to make the hard decisions. To lead. To not make mistakes.

I felt the shame snake its insidious tendrils through my being.

"There was an awful snowstorm in Chicago. Twenty-two inches fell in less than twenty-four hours. They called it *Snowmageddon*. As the last of the snow petered off, the entire area plunged into the coldest temperatures I'd ever witnessed. In the negative sixties with the windchill. It made for a very long shift—stuck in the emergency room. We couldn't leave because the cases never stopped coming. And we were stuck even if we could clock off—because the roads were a mess.

"It was thirty-six hours with just short stints of sleep here and there before trauma events. There was an accident —three passengers. I'm not sure where they'd been going in a blizzard—but they were driving down Lake Shore Drive and careened off the highway into Lake Michigan. So we were battling hypothermia and level one traumatic events in the patients.

"They gave me the worst of the cases. The driver. A woman. In her early twenties. Her body had been crushed by the steering shaft. We did everything we could. There was so much bleeding and damage from her rib cage and pelvis. It was a difficult decision. It always is. But eventually it becomes obvious the only thing keeping them alive are the machines—and someone, usually the head trauma surgeon—me at the time—has to make the call to end lifesaving efforts and notify the family and speak to them about organ donation.

"We were all exhausted. Those nights are the hardest because it's a never-ending parade of awful tragedies. One after the other. The organ extraction team came in and began to prep her. My head nurse thought she saw her hand move. Insisted, in fact, she'd seen it. Told everyone I made the call too early.

"We'd worked together a long time. The nurse and me. She was without a doubt as astute, knowledgeable, and medically capable as I was. But every single time I replay it in my head, I do a rundown of all the signs we look for in a case where we need to make the call to end lifesaving measures. And she checked every box. Every single one. But we were all also exhausted.

"Word spread fast. We were called before our administrators. Things got ugly. I'm not an innocent party. Getting to that level of success forces you to be almost arrogant in how self-assured one is. And, when that experience or know how is challenged..? I didn't handle it well. I lashed out to cover my own feelings of self-doubt and recrimination.

"The story got leaked to the press. It ended up on the news. It was a very dark moment in my life and career. I didn't lose my license, but I don't know if anyone in Chicago would ever hire me again, even if I hadn't stolen away to my mentor's cabin in the woods.

"I found peace in Sycamore Mountain. No one knew who I was. I had zero expectations on my shoulders. I could just exist for a while. Except, everyone in town was so fucking cheery and neighborly and, in my business, I couldn't handle it when I was an open, oozing, festering wound. So I hid out in the house. During one of my sleepless nights, I was watching a documentary on bourbon and remembered spending some time with my friend Pat at his family distillery and starting noodling with mash recipes. Before I knew it, I created my first bourbon batch."

I felt like I'd been talking forever. In fact, my voice was hoarse from the effort of expelling those demons. Somewhere in my story, Remle had snaked her way to the head of my bed, mimicking my position on the bed. She smiled but said nothing, so I continued.

"Bourbon distilling takes a lot of knowledge and skills I'd use in medicine—chemistry, reaction times, researching what combination delivers the best results. But does so with zero pressure. It was exactly what I needed. No decision was life or death. If something didn't work, I just threw it out and started over again."

She'd been spot on when she said tragedy sometimes brings the best things. Lakshmi saved me. It provided me some semblance of peace when my whole world felt like it was being torn apart.

thirteen

Remle.

There were words of comfort I wanted to speak. Sometimes though, the best way to honor someone's suffering is to give the exorcised story the freedom to dissipate without distraction. His pain was a palpable presence in the room. I could feel it as if it had a pulse and a heartbeat. While our stories weren't exact, they were similar enough, I understood it, how tortured you can become with the pain.

I'd become so engrossed in his story and giving him the space to decide how much he wanted to say, I completely missed the knocking on the door.

"Are you expecting anyone?" Jasper shoved off the bed and jogged to the door.

"Oh, hi!" I heard Gemini's voice carry into the room. "I'm just dropping these off for Remle."

She stood in front of me faster than I expected, a handful of dresses slung over her shoulder.

"I wasn't sure what you'd be comfortable with, so I

pulled all the ones I had. Do you want me to leave them all and pick them up after dinner?"

"Sure. Yeah. That would be great. Thank you again for this."

"It's not a problem. I'm so sorry they didn't have anything at the resort. You would think in this day and age they'd be more size-inclusive. I'll speak to Penn about it. Not specifically about this. Just in general, in a conversation at some point." She offloaded the dresses onto the wardrobe rack.

"Great! Well, I need to grab a shower, so we'll see you downstairs at seven, right?"

I barely knew the woman who had just shown a massive kindness toward me. But I needed to be finished with this conversation about how I was too fat to fit into the clothes at the gift shop. Especially in front of Jasper. I didn't need him bearing witness to my biggest insecurities right at the onset of what could potentially be a relationship.

I couldn't make eye contact with him. I rustled around in my bag, grabbed what I needed for a shower, as well as three of the dresses she'd given as options, and rushed into the bathroom without another word. I prayed the exchange would be forgotten by the time I finished.

"All set!" I said way too brightly to even sound genuine.

Jasper sat on the couch, legs splayed, relaxed as he flipped through channels on the television. He'd taken a shower after me, and my blood still vibrated with the sight of Jasper wrapped just in a towel, strutting across the hotel room to his bag.

He had a tattoo on his chest over his heart in the most beautiful script. I didn't have enough time to stare at it to make it out before he walked back into the bathroom to finish getting dressed. It didn't mean the rest of the time we'd spent getting ready I hadn't stopped thinking about it —or all of the muscles in his long, lean body.

He looked ridiculously dapper in jeans and a polo shirt. How he could effortlessly pull off casual yet elegant with just a shower was beyond me. Meanwhile, I'd tried on all of Gemini's dresses, debating whether I should fake a stomach bug and not attend.

"Hey." We stood waiting for the elevators to arrive at our floor. He directed my chin up to meet his gaze. "I think you're stunning. Regardless of the size on the tag of that dress."

He waved me in when the elevator arrived seconds later, and as the doors closed, pulled me in for a kiss. The word *kiss* didn't even do the action justice. It was poetry. A sonnet written with dips, swoops, and curls across every insecurity I'd drown myself in over the course of the day. It last less than a second, but in my head we'd span the universe, floating above space and time, locked in our own bubble of exploration.

"Don't let the inventory in some mountain resort define your self-worth. You are an amazing woman. A total package, in and out." He kissed my hand, locking gazes with mine, refusing to look away. There were unspoken paragraphs in the depths of his chocolate-colored eyes. He smiled at me before guiding my hand down against his pants. The move both stunned me silent, while setting off a cacophony of feelings and sensations inside my body.

"You're looking at me as if I'm lying to you. This doesn't lie."

He held my hand and pressed it harder against the very pronounced ridge in his jeans. I wanted to explore. To open up my palm and stretch my fingers. I wished we could return to the hotel room and continue what he'd started.

"Dinnertime," he whispered against my ear as the elevator dinged, announcing we arrived on the ground floor.

"Wait, a second. How can you work *for the Bourbon Association* and not drink bourbon?" Gemini slapped her hand on the table in a fit of giggles.

The evening's dinner seemed to be the perfect salve after an afternoon of opening up our deepest wounds and airing them. The entire table of Gemini's guests was fun, hilarious, and such a delight to be around. Even Jasper appeared to have come out of his shell.

"I'm not a big drinker." I shrugged. I felt the heat rising on my cheeks as the whole table's focus landed on me.

"You went to U.K." Jasper turned, his voice raised a half octave.

I had no idea how he knew.

"Because they have an awesome basketball team—and honestly, if you grow up in Kentucky, it's like written in your DNA you attend."

"I don't know Jasper," Emmett pointed his thumb in my direction, "as the owner of one of the best bourbons I've personally ever tasted. How is this possible?"

"Duane!" Finn called to the chef, who approached with

another round of dessert, "Could you please ask your bartender to bring a tasting flight of bourbons for the table?"

"Ooooh, looks like Finn has decided today is the day to school you little grasshopper." Emmett hooted.

"If we could get Lakshmi V, a 1792, the Basil Hayden's, the Old Forester, and the Knob Creek—if you don't have enough of those for the table, we can do a Woodford, the Four Roses small batch, or a Russell's Reserve." Jasper rattled off more bourbons than I thought humanly possible to know.

While I didn't technically drink bourbons, I at least knew who my clients were and who the up and comers were. Jasper's knowledge of high quality bourbon at all price points was impressive. The rest of the table seemed equally fascinated, some of them even referring to the back of the spirits' menu to do their own research.

"Let's start with the Knob Creek." He held up the miniature sipping glass. I thought so the rest of the table knew which he selected, but instead he brought it to my lips. "Knob Creek is considered a gateway bourbon. It's affordable, accessible, straightforward."

"It burns," Amelia hissed as she cleared her glass.

"Definitely not my favorite," Gemini agreed. "This one is probably better mixed with something like a julep or a Manhattan."

"What do you think?" Jasper asked.

He was so close to me. I could feel his breath warm against my cheek. His nearness tickled up my spine, insinuated itself into my circulatory system.

"It's too intense," I told him. "The oakiness is overwhelming."

The chef placed a dessert in front of us. Jasper gathered some of the whipped cream on his spoon and fed it to me.

"This will cut down on the bitterness in the back of your throat."

While I tried to cleanse my palate, he picked up the next glass.

"Smell the inside of your glass from the Knob Creek. You can smell the barrel, the oakiness, the grassy scent of the trees. It presents very clean and fresh. As Gemini said, a perfect mixing bourbon. The Basil Hayden and the 1792 will present similarly in regard to bold flavors. Neither has a lot of subtlety, but they are both easy sipping bourbons."

Somehow being with Jasper made tasting bourbon a wholly erotic experience. If it wasn't his throaty whisper sending shivers up my spine, it was the gentle tickle of his fingers against mine when I took a glass from him. That brief moment of contact raising gooseflesh on my arms and skittering sensation through every nerve ending. And his assessing gaze every time I sipped from my glass felt intimate. Like it was just him and me and I was his private student.

"The Old Forester is an experience in all the senses," Jasper announced to the table. "Smell." He instructed just to me. "Tell me what you think is in there."

It wasn't anything like the previous two.

"It smells like the inside of a bakery. It's spicy—but also kind of fruity. But also, it smells like cake batter," I told him, and the table agreed.

"Now take a very tiny sip and roll it around on your tongue for a few seconds before you swallow. Tell me how it finishes."

This one went down like a dream. There was no bite. No

sharpness in the back of my throat or burning up into my sinuses.

"What do you taste gorgeous?" He pushed away a strand of hair and held me by the jaw.

His lips look so kissable. A little dewy form the sip of bourbon, that baked goods smell lingering between the two of us. I leaned forward just enough to close the distance between us. I couldn't take it anymore. The mounting sizzle that twisted with each smile, caress, or intimate whisper had me squirming.

Fuck it. I said to myself. I didn't even care we had an entire table as our audience. I leaned in, caressing my lips against his in open invitation. I wanted to *be* kissed. By him. To have him take possession of my mouth and lay claim. The suggestion was all he needed. The moment our lips connected, he made a study of every peak and valley of my mouth. Exploring as if he were an explorer charting new territory.

"You." I smiled when we came up for air. "Oh and some cherries too. Perhaps a subtle hint of chocolate."

There was heat in his eyes. I saw it. Despite the darkened room, and the deep brown color of his eyes, something flared in them signaling he wanted to kiss me again and again. I wanted it too. A thousand kisses. The breath stealing kind. The ones where you became so absorbed in the sensation the world just melted away.

"Penn, you may want to get those smoke detectors checked. I don't know about the rest of you but Jesus...that was fucking fire." Emmett shook his fingers as if his hand were burning.

The table erupted into a chorus of snickers, hoots, and hollers. Perhaps I underestimated just how magnetic Jasper was. All I wanted to do was keep kissing him, maybe even while we shifted to a horizontal position.

"I saved the best for last." He held up the glass with his own bourbon in it, putting it against my lips. "Sip. And hold it in your mouth. Roll it around on your tongue. Take a deep breath through your nose while it settles into the recess of your mouth. Then swallow."

Warm. That's what I felt. Everywhere. Warmth on my face. Warmth down my throat and heating my chest. Warmth from the inside.

I did as Jasper said. I followed each of his steps. The taste of his bourbon reminded me of a chai tea—but a boozy version.

"I got cinnamon right away," I tell him. "A little clove. It feels like a chai tea, to be honest."

"She has a great palate," Gemini told Jasper. "It's subtle, but it definitely presents with a lot of chai notes with a lovely caramel-vanilla finish."

"I like this one best. And not just because the distiller is easy on the eyes."

Jasper ran his finger across my lip, as if that digit stored all the memories of what our kiss felt like moments ago. He downed his own glass of bourbon before turning to me and kissing me a second time. This one was much gentler than the first. When the first drop of bourbon entered my mouth, I understood why he'd been so gentle. He fed me drop after drop of bourbon from his tongue, caressing it into my mouth. I don't know if I would ever want to drink bourbon another way, ever again.

"Well friends, I think the James Beard nominated chef has tuckered herself out amid all the excitement," Finn announced to the table.

Gemini's head rested on his shoulder, the brightest smile lighting up her face.

"Thank you for coming." She told the room, not moving her head from where it lay. "I honestly can't believe our little tavern has achieved so much in such a small amount of time. I'm speechless, honestly. And I have so much love for you Finn, for never saying no to any crazy idea I have. And Emmett, you truly are my right-hand man, and I couldn't have done any of it without you."

"Thank god I lost my left one," Emmett quipped, "or you seriously would have been fucked."

The entire table burst out in loud laughter. I liked him a lot. He was charming and funny, and shit if I didn't just sit in awe of his outlook on his situation.

"Can you just bring the dresses by in the morning?" Gemini asked, as everyone stood.

I was so distracted with nodding my agreement, I somehow missed her leaning in to pull me into a hug. We'd arrived at friendly hugs. The whole table. We all parted in the same way. It was as if I'd become one of them.

fourteen

Jasper

There was a war going on inside of me. Part of me wanted to take Remle by the hand, drag her caveman style up to the room and ravage her. On the opposing side of my desire, I wanted to lay her out on the bed and take my time learning every way to make her moan and sigh. Then, of course, the gentleman in me wanted to find some place quiet, have another drink, and learn everything there was to learn about Remle Clay from Lexington.

Perhaps it was the wine with dinner, and the five-flight bourbon tasting, but Remle enthralled me in so many ways. Even saying her name felt like a kiss against my soft palate. I wanted to be infused with her. To distill all of her complexities into a recipe only I fully understood. I was drunk on Remle Clay, and I didn't know if I ever wanted to sober up.

"You are something else, Ms. Clay."

"Oh?" She leaned her head against the wall of the

elevator and turned her head toward me. "What exactly about me is something else?"

I wanted to push her against the elevator wall and kiss her. My body ached with the need. The ride was too short to gain any satisfaction from, however, and before I could even answer her question, we arrived at our floor.

"I looked you up on LinkedIn," I tell her, the drinks with dinner were apparently a truth serum. "After you left Lakshmi when you pulled your coup with Iris. You looked so pleased with yourself. As if you'd mounted a general-level strategy and had me surrounded. I wanted to learn more about you."

"And did you learn everything you needed to, Mr. Raj?" She walked backward toward our room, her curls bouncing against her shoulders as we walked.

"Magna Cum Laude graduate, double major in journalism and P.R. and apparently an adept equestrian based on your headshot."

"Actually, I hate horses." She giggled. "But Kentucky is horses and bourbon. I wanted a job close to home so, I pandered."

She raised her arms in the air as if telling the whole world to fuck off.

"You are much friendlier and approachable than people think you are," she told me, wrapping her arms around my neck. "You should let others see this side of you. It's really nice."

I didn't have a response. Scratch that, I had a lot of responses, but they were all sexual in nature and total come ons. Since I still vacillated between learning more about her in the personal or biblical sense, I held my tongue.

"Okay, so you have to promise me." She pushed against

my chest as I unlocked the door to our room. "You are not allowed to laugh or make any comment about my pajamas. I didn't think anyone but me would see me in them."

"Well now, I'm intrigued."

Her eyes widened and a perfect "o" formed on her lips. Her perfect, kissable lips. I wanted to taste them again. More than once.

"I promise," I told her, crossing my chest, "no judgments on your sleepwear. You can't judge me either."

"Why are you wearing like SpongeBob shorts or something to bed?"

Her hair hung over her face as she bent to collect her clothes to take into the bathroom. I was desperate to run my hand through it. To feel its softness against my fingers and breathe in the fruity scent of her shampoo.

"No, I sleep in the nude."

Remle lay in the next bed, sleeping in a ratty old university T-shirt. While there is absolutely nothing wrong with sleeping in old T-shirts, it was the mental image of her coming out of the shower, smelling like steam and soap, in said shirt that had me at full mast. Also, I hadn't been kidding about sleeping in the nude. My stiff cock brushed against my hand every time I shifted on the mattress. Every whisper of fabric caressing the sensitive head had me considering going into the bathroom.

Her shirt was so old and well-worn, I could clearly make out the turgid, raspberry peaks of her breasts. I couldn't get the image out of my head. In fact, every time I thought I finally forgot about them, I'd lick my lips, or swallow and my brain would play all kinds of tawdry images of taking those breasts into my mouth and suckling.

"That's the fifth time you've sighed."

Remle's voice danced across the silence of the room.

"You can't sleep either?" she asked.

She was too precious for me. All of her concern. The well of empathy that Remle possessed was too deep for her to actually be human. Remle was like Marvel universe level empathetic.

"No," I admitted. It was best to keep the answer simple. Otherwise she'd ask why ,and I had no idea what to tell her then.

"Me either."

I heard the sheets rustle and glanced across the room. In the dim moonlight and the artificial glow from the clock radio, I could see her staring at me. I turned and mimicked her pose. My stiff cock, uncomfortably situated between my legs, needed to be repositioned twice before it felt even moderately comfortable.

"Did you mean what you said earlier?" she asked me across the crevasse of space between us.

I ran through all of our conversations from throughout the night. Trying to suss out which conversation had led to any confusion. I came up empty.

"Which thing are you unsure of?"

"When you said you were attracted to me."

Was she kidding? I rewound the entire evening to re-evaluate any time over the past few hours, where I hadn't made my attraction to her fully apparent. I couldn't find a single moment.

"Placing your hand on my cock and kissing you with abandon wasn't clear enough for you?"

"Oh no, those were *plenty* clear. But then we got back here, and well—we're in separate beds and I thought for sure we'd at least get each other off. I just assumed something must have happened between downstairs and us going to bed."

"I was trying to be a gentleman."

"Oh," I heard her whisper.

"We're in a room together. We only moderately know one another. Despite the kissing, I didn't want to assume."

She didn't reply for so long I thought she fell asleep. Silence hung between us as thick as the darkness that surrounded us. I heard her sigh, fluff her pillow, and settle back into position, still facing me.

I took a chance. I didn't give myself time to second guess the decision. I stretched over my head for the lamp and clicked it on.

"Remle," she locked eyes with me when I said her name, "this should leave absolutely no room for misinterpretation."

fifteen

Remle.

He really did sleep in the nude. It was the first thought shotgunning through my mind. And then, the only thing in my mind was the long, hard cock proudly jutting from a thick thatch of pubic hair. I couldn't stop staring.

"I've been hard for you since the gallery," he admitted. "I haven't been able to stop thinking about you, actually. But I also didn't want you to think I invited you here just to get in your pants. I honestly want you to talk to Gemini tomorrow."

"Jasper?"

My mouth felt dry. Suddenly, I couldn't catch my breath. The more he talked, the more I wondered if I was in fact crazy to want to feel him between my legs—after having just met three days prior.

My eyes progressed with great difficulty back up to his face. A cocky smile splayed across his lips. He rolled to his back, cock in hand, as if he knew I couldn't stop staring.

"No more talk of Gemini," I told him.

"Agreed."

He slowly manipulated his cock, pushing his foreskin up and down. I marveled at the progression of colors from umber to rose as the glistening tip was revealed and hidden with each jerk of his cock. I'd never seen an uncircumcised cock before. Not to say I was a cock expert. But the few I'd seen bore the mushroomed tops of circumcision.

"C'mere."

I scrambled out of my bed, and into his with a graceful efficiency I never thought I possessed.

"Closer. I want to see those gorgeous tits of yours teasing me through your top. You can thank that rag of a T-shirt for this." He nodded toward his stiff cock with a smile.

I tugged at the hem, preparing to bring it over my head, when he stayed my hand.

"No, leave it on. Just the hint of those beauties is turning me on."

Rather than oblige, I leaned toward him so he could get a view straight down. I saw he was so distracted by the hint of what he'd been given a peek at his hand stopped rubbing his cock. Just above his hand, I explored his skin with a long, slow lick from shaft to tip. Once at the top, I enveloped my lips around his tip, bathing him with my tongue.

He wrapped his arm around my midsection and yanked me toward him. Yanked me. With a single arm and repositioned me so my ass was on full display in his face.

"Turnabout is fair play."

He lifted me by my legs across his chest. He spread them, one on either side of his head. I knew what was coming. My body crackled with awareness at his proximity. I felt his breath on my thighs, his fingers tickling along the elastic banding of my panties. Rather than yank them down as I thought he would, he ran his fingers beneath the cheap cotton, caressing the smooth skin of my southern lips. Each pass of his fingers had my hips moving in desperation to catch his fingers and direct them to where I needed him most.

I sucked him harder, bringing more of him into my mouth, teasing against the back of my throat. He was larger than I'd expected—or had experience with—especially in the oral department. But everything I did was rewarded by a shift in his hips, or a groan of satisfaction.

The thing it didn't reward me for was any kind of friction against my own throbbing little nub. It had been desperate for relief since the first time Jasper kissed me. And I wanted him to kiss me again. Except on my other lips.

No sooner had I thought about my wish, he had my panties pulled to the side and had buried himself between my legs. The first passing swipe of his tongue had me seeing stars. His fingers joined the party, gently stroking in and out, making a map of my insides. Count on the doctor to know exactly what he sought and reach it with precise efficiency.

His fingers pressed against my g-spot, alternating between soft and hard presses in concert with his sensual attack on my clit. The combination had been wantonly pressing against his mouth, desperate for the release teasing just out of reach but builing like a freight train.

The quicker I climbed, the faster I tried to keep up. Jasper and I were a symphony of pleasure, sighing, groaning, giving, receiving, on an infinite loop. I wanted more. I didn't want to come like this. I'd always been a one and done kind of girl, and I really wanted to experience what it felt like to have Jasper inside of me.

"Condom?" I asked, hoping as a former doctor he might have some kind of ingrained desire to always be prepared.

Jasper doubled down, feasting on me like it was his last meal. In mere seconds, I reached the point of no return. I fell over into a bliss stretched out in infinite waves. Boneless. Near blind with pleasure. Unable to form a coherent thought, I barely registered the bed move.

"I wonder if Gemini will notice I swiped a rubber from her clinic." Jasper wiggled his eyebrows at me, taking my leg and positioning it up by his head. He ran his fingers along the inside, making me squirm with delight. "Gosh, you're so beautiful right now. Your cheeks are flushed, and your eyes are such a bright blue. Lift up your shirt. Let me see your breasts. I bet they're gorgeous, too."

I honestly forgot I still wore a shirt. It went over my head in an instant. It was just enough time, however, for Jasper to line himself up and push into me. We both writhed and gyrated at the sensation of him slowly filling me. It had been a while since I'd had actual flesh inside of me, and it took a moment to get used to being filled. The stretch, however, was divine.

I existed in a cloud of bliss. With each soft caress or whispered compliment, it twisted a cloud into a tornado of need. Jasper shifted, placing his forearms on either side of me, looking me in the eyes while he continued to move inside me. His lips left trails of liquid heat everywhere they found purchase. Across my lips, down my jaw, on both of my nipples which he pulled against and nipped. I wanted everything all at once. I never wanted it to end, while concurrently racing toward a summit I hadn't thought possible to achieve a second time.

"We should do this again very soon," Jasper suggested,

taking a nip at my earlobe. "I don't know how much longer this is going to last."

We could do it over and again for infinity for all I cared. It felt too good. I wanted to feel like that forever. To only exist in mindless, voiceless, sightless, ecstasy.

I fell over seconds later, in a spasm of muscles and a scream of apogee. I was certain the entire floor heard. Jasper followed a few moments later, collapsing across me as he came down.

"I can't promise I'll recover fast enough to do that again tonight." Jasper brushed aside my hair to place a gentle kiss on my lips. "But we are most certainly doing that again."

He'd hear no arguments from me.

sixteen

Jasper

"What does your tattoo mean?"

We took our time getting out of bed. After an unexpected but undeniably pleasurable evening, and a repeat this morning, we were trying to find the motivation to get out of bed and head over to the Tavern.

"*Media vita in morte sumus, memento vivere,*" I tell her. "In the midst of our lives, we die. Remember to live."

I felt her nails trace the swooping script, pulling a shiver from me. Her hair was like silk between my fingers. The way the sun played in her hair had been so captivating, I hadn't been able to stop playing with it.

"That quote is very you."

"It's a good thing, since it's kind of permanent." I chuckled before accepting her kiss.

Earlier in the early morning haze, before I'd been fully awake, I'd thought about Remle in comparison to past relationships, and how despite this one being in its infancy, it *felt* different. Of course, I wasn't in the same place mentally or emotionally as I'd been as a doctor. I was a completely different person now, but I couldn't ever remember just luxuriating in the press of a soft body against mine. Taking every opportunity possible to kiss and being present in those subtle exchanges. It was nice. This quiet, reflective space I found myself in with Remle.

"We better shake a leg." I tapped her on the ass, which was a mistake. The moment my hand came in contact with her lush rump, I desperately wanted to explore once again.

"You're going to start something and then be all '*Remle, I told you we have to get going*' when I show you how much I love your hands there."

"Shower, clothes. Gemini is making us brunch. The faster we get ready, the sooner we get to gorge ourselves on James Beard Award level food."

"I thought about what you told me yesterday." Gemini hadn't stopped putting food in front of us. The amount she'd prepared, her and Emmett, had to have been up cooking since around the time Remle and I went in for round two.

"Taste the oatmeal first." She pushed two ramekins in our direction. "It's essentially the same principles of a mash. There's wheat, barely, and cornmeal. Not apples to apples, but the same flavor profiles."

"To the oatmeal, I added some of your suggestions. There're blackberries, cinnamon, a hint of turmeric, coriander, and some blood orange to add some acid to both balance the coriander and brighten its lemony flavor."

"This is fantastic." Remle savored every bite, just as she had the bourbon the night before. I hadn't told her why I asked Gemini to come up with flavor profiles, but she was a smart cookie. I'm sure if she hadn't already surmised our intent, she would before our tasting was finished.

"I really like it." I made notes in the book I'd brought with me. "The bright citrus makes it feel almost floral. I think I know which one this will be."

"I'm so glad you did! I think I know which one it is. Can I guess?" Gemini clapped her hands together and danced in place.

"Can we present all the flavor profiles first, *then* you can play guess the label?" Emmett ruffled his hand in her bun before playfully pushing her out of the way.

"Let me present them. I'll be much quicker than you are. They haven't got the rest of the week, you know. It's at least four hours back to North Carolina."

Gemini swatted his hand away with a laugh before continuing.

"Fine. So the second one is clove, star anise, cinnamon, cherries, and dark chocolate."

"Mm, this one feels rich and kind of sinful." Remle shook her head while she scooped up a second spoonful to taste. "Hedonistic in a way."

"I like the description."

Gemini passed us each a little saucer of lemon sorbet so we could cleanse our palates before the next taste. I made notes on her second recipe and how I would pair it. I desperately wanted to know how Remle saw the puzzle coming together, but also wanted her to be at my home in my laboratory to experience these all in real time.

It was then it hit me Remle wasn't permanent to North Carolina. Obviously in the back of my head I knew it, logically. But I wanted to ingratiate her into my decision process. To seek her advice, welcome her into my confidences.

"Okay, the next two have a heavy caramel base. I know it diverges a bit from your Indian roots, but I wanted to make sure the four bottles were separate, but distinct."

I glanced over at Remle, and her whole face lit up. Her lips quirked into a smile she would force straight, only to quirk into a smile once again. Fuck, she was adorable.

"Something you'd like to say, Ms. Clay?"

Gemini hid her snicker behind her wrist, trying to cover it with a fake cough.

"No, nothing of importance." She cocked her sassy little eyebrow at me. I watched her try to force a smile from appearing on her face. A valiant effort that she presently failed at.

"Oh, I thought maybe you'd noticed something. Perhaps something Gemini said might have sent you down a path."

"You mean the one where you decided to take my suggestion and offer accessible versions of Lakshmi? That one?"

"I'd say it is in fact, the one, yes."

"Yeah, how about that?" Her hand sat on the hip she'd jutted out with a mock attitude. "The obnoxious little salesperson who couldn't possibly have anything to interest you gives you an all-star level idea."

"You wanna keep crowing like a rooster before dawn, or how about I tell you my vision?"

I took her by the hand and guided her into my lap. She wrapped her arms around me and pulled me in for a kiss.

"Tell me I had a good idea." She vibrated with so much excitement she practically hooted as she spoke. "I want to hear you say your local Bourbon Association rep provided you with exceptional insight and has demonstrated her value to the Lakshmi brand."

"Oh, she is exceptional for sure." I ran my hand up her haunches, pinching her ass and making her giggle. "And as far as her value to the Lakshmi brand. I'd say she's been quite adept at anticipating the needs of Lakshmi and servicing each one of those needs with enthusiasm."

"Okay guys, seriously, get a room. We've all been there. The fun, fanciful early days of a relationship. But Gemini rarely makes her sticky buns and I'm not going to ruin this day by upending my breakfast because of you two carrying on like teenagers desperate to find a parking spot to neck." Emmett pushed the next sample ramekin in front of both of us, chuckling at his joke. "Eat up. You've only got two left, then you can get on the road and go find a turnoff to get in each other's pants."

"We'll be making four single year varieties. I'm going to base them off my four paintings: *Padmasana*, which is the Lotus, *Utphallaka*, which is Blossom, *Indranika*, the Queen of Heaven, and *Kissan*, the peasant."

"Please tell me the bottles will look like the paintings." Remle turned to me, those sapphire jewels she had for eyes, echoing the same excitement I felt for this new concept. "Holy shit, Jasper! This is going to put you on every map. It's going to be huge."

That's what I was hoping for. Remle's idea had been a stroke of genius, quite honestly. Not only did it disrupt the single year market with affordable, accessible, yet sexy. But it also allowed for fun and experimentation with very low risk.

"Gemini has been diligently studying the four poses—"

"In more ways than one." Finn winked at her, sneaking in to grab a sticky bun, and taking a seat on the other side of the counter.

Gemini blushed clear up to her hairline.

"Matching flavor profiles to the emotion of the paintings has been so fun. Honestly, Remle, your idea really was—to use a totally apropos term the kids are using—a chef's kiss kind of idea."

It had been a lot harder than I thought to say goodbye to Gemini and company. The visit, despite only lasting twenty-four hours, served as a reminder of a past me I'd lost connection to. I liked being around people. Conversation, exchanging ideas, hearing other people's perspectives— were all things I significantly lacked of late. Sure, I had Meadow and Gavin, and I shot the shit with the Lakshmi team when they came for distilling and packaging stints. But other than a few friends I still kept in contact with in Chicago, I didn't really have anyone close by.

My reclusion had always been a self-imposed kind of solitary confinement. As if removing myself from living life could serve as penance for what happened to Antonia Hastings. That was her name. It haunted me, always. In medicine, necessity typically drown out those kinds of personal details from your mind. Especially while you were operating. One needed to remain somewhat detached, otherwise the job ate you from the inside.

Once it leaked to the press, there was no escaping her name, even if I wanted to. Not only did I know her name, I knew what she looked like. Not just her, mind you, but her mom and dad, her kids, her siblings. They all haunted me. The videos of them sobbing into the cameras demanding answers. I wanted answers, too. They'd never come—and I'd forever carry her ghost on my shoulder.

seventeen

Remle

"Your friends are pretty great."

Gemini, Amelia, and I already had a group chat established. The pair planned to come up and see me in Lexington. I already had a zoom on my calendar for the following week to talk to Gemini about a P.R. plan for her clinic.

"This visit was unexpected, but in the best way." Jasper leaned his temple against the arm propped against the window.

He had a faraway look in his eyes suggesting he was lost down memory lane, but there was the smallest upturn in his lips hinting toward good memories.

"I owe so much to Gemini. I don't know if I ever told you. It was her who brought Lakshmi into Chef Tobin's restaurant and started serving it with desserts, offering specialty drinks with it—over and again until people started requesting it by name. She was a one-woman promoter of my brand, and it took off like a rocket thanks to her."

"I'm not discounting anything Gemini did, because she's

awesome, but don't undervalue your own talent. Your bourbon is really good. Honestly. If someone had given it to me in last night's flight, totally blind, and asked me to pick out the one from the baby distillery—it wouldn't have been yours I selected. Distilling takes talent, patience, skill, so many things need to come together for a perfect batch—and for you to tap into it so early in your practice. It's pretty amazing."

The drive back to North Carolina seemed to go much faster. I felt like I blinked, and we were halfway home. Jasper and I chatted about everything and nothing simultaneously. I heard about his sister in California, his parents, who struggled with boredom now that they'd retired. How he was learning about Hinduism and really felt connected to which Catholicism hadn't.

I told him about my brother and my little niece. What a struggle it was to get to see her, given her mom and maternal grandparents lived in Elizabethtown, which was some ways away. I wanted her to feel connected to us, to get to know pieces of her dad, and also feel like me and my parents were her family as well.

Shep: Haven't had a check-in lately.
Shep: Gimme good news

Ugh. Of all people. He was the last person I wanted breaking our pleasant little bubble.

Me: With Jasper now. I'll keep you updated.

Shep: Tick tock Remle.

There were pieces about my job I loved. People, the social events, helping plan campaigns and advise our members on how they could better market themselves. Shep, however, he was too much.

"What a sigh." Jasper reach across the arm rest and caressed my knee.

"My boss. He's driving me bonkers." My cell phone clattered into the cup holder as I dropped it in.

"Ah. I'd completely forgotten you were attempting to woo me."

"Did it work?"

I gave him a saucy smirk and fluffed my hair, earning me the sexiest belly laugh. It was the first time he rewarded me with a genuine, unfiltered laugh, and I wanted more. Sure, I heard him laughing and carrying on with Gemini and company yesterday. But this laugh was because of me and directed toward me. His arctic shell was melting and every now and again I'd get a peek of the warm, genial man existed beneath. I wanted more of him.

"I guess you'll have to wait and see." He ran his hand around his mouth, almost as if he couldn't believe he presently smiled and laughed either.

"Sometimes the best things are the ones you have to wait the longest for."

"You haven't seen much of Lakshmi other than the two front rooms." Jasper cut the engine to his truck, the lights of the cabin slowly adjusting in brightness until we were both bathed in amber light.

Somewhere along the time we crossed state borders, I'd nodded off and woken up as he pulled into Lakshmi.

"I can make some dinner," he offered, "and show you around. It's quite peaceful here right now. The calm before the bottling storm sits just on the horizon."

"You cook?" I asked, trying hard to school the surprise in my features.

"I'm no Gemini Tate, but I know my way around a kitchen. What do you say? Are you game?"

"Always."

He led me through the main entrance, all the lights glowing in welcome as we approached.

"It's probably better to see the operational side of things in the daylight, so a grounds tour will have to be saved for another day. My residence is just up here off the main hall."

We walked up a set of wood floating stairs into an open loft. I don't know why I was surprised the Zen interior from downstairs in its riverstone, greenery, and wood continued upstairs as well. The space was super modern, but in a soothing, luxe way.

"Has Gemini seen this kitchen?"

It was the kitchen of daydreams. Gigantic chef's quality appliances, double hi-tech refrigerators, and swanky, ebony wood round table large enough to make King Arthur swoon.

"Who do you think ordered all of this for me?"

"She apparently thinks you're quite popular. What is this? An eighteen person table?"

"No, it sits fourteen—ten comfortably."

"I don't think I even know fourteen people to invite to a dinner party."

Jasper pulled out a chair for me, which I took before padding to his wine fridge.

"Well, between the crew we just met—that's fourteen right there. It doesn't even include the extended friends. From what Gemini has relayed lately, Penn's wife is a famous radio host. Typically, wherever she and Penn go, her co-host and his wife go as well. They're pretty much tied at the hip."

He set a bright, fruity wine in front of me, along with a plate of cheeses and fruits he'd whipped together with little effort. He clearly kept much better food in stock than I did. If I tried to whip up an appetizer with what was presently in my fridge, he'd get some pickles of questionable freshness, a container of single serve guacamole, maybe some yogurt, and potentially, depending on the day, a bagged salad.

"Yes, but those are all your friends."

"They're *your* friends as well now. I saw you texting with Gemini on the way home. You're already thick as thieves."

"We were." I laughed into my wineglass, remembering all the inappropriate chatter between the three of us about Jasper and our *extracurricular* activities. I'm not one to kiss and tell—but when the kissing happened in public, it required at least a little of telling.

"Having girlfriend chatter? It's something I've missed."

"Did you and your friends have a falling out, then?" Jasper asked over the clang of pots and pans.

Despite having gone to a large college and immersing myself in sorority life, I found once we'd scattered to our new corners of the world, maintaining those friendships became much harder. Especially when everyone's life plan began moving at different speeds. My plan still seemed to be in neutral.

"We all just kind of lost contact." I didn't know how to explain it. We liked each other's posts on Instagram. Commented the occasional *so cute!* Or *so happy for you!* But we weren't connected. Not in the way we used to be.

"This is a Pea Pulau," he set the most fragrant platter of rice between us, "along with a red lentil dal, and some naan."

"This is super impressive."

I dug in with fervor. Given the last time we ate real food was Gemini's breakfast, I was famished with a capital F. It could have been the hunger talking, but Jasper's cooking was swoon worthy.

"Are you sure you aren't a professional chef too?" I teased, using the naan the mop up the last of my dal. "Did Gemini send you home with all of this food and you're just making a bunch of noise over the shaking empty pots and pans to cover up the sound of the microwave?"

"Busted." He held his hands up, hiding his laughter behind a closed fist. "It was my mom. When she comes down to visit, she cooks the entire time she's here. I actually had to buy an oversized freezer in my garage to hold all the food she cooked for me."

"I don't know whether to commend your honesty, be

salty you tried to trick me, or be impressed you almost convinced me. Smooth Mr. Raj, very smooth."

"I can cook." He assured me over a sip of wine, "It would take much longer than twenty minutes and given we drove through and didn't stop for lunch, I was famished and figured you would be too."

"You guessed right. And your mom is an amazing cook."

"Meadow said the paintings are installed. Let's go check them out before I show you something special."

"If you're going to show me your cock, I've already seen it," I quipped.

It was the glass of wine. I'm easily a two drink drunk. The shocked look on Jasper's face tickled me even more than my original joke.

"Hold tight two seconds." He jogged to the back of the loft, I assumed, toward his bedroom, and returned in a flash with a pair of towels. "This is for later."

We went down a different set of stairs from the ones we'd gone up. This one deposited us into a room I'd not yet seen overlooking the back of the grounds: the distilling barn, the grain fields, and the warehouse. The room looked educational, in purpose. A long black stone island ran the length of the oversized room. Each side of the island was dotted with chairs, and shelves hung on each of the walls with various Lakshmi bottles.

"Is this another tasting room?" I asked as we stepped off the stairs and into the space.

"Not quite. Think of it as a demonstration room. It's also a testing room. Next week when we're fully staffed, we'll cook our mash in here. Sometimes it acts as a test kitchen, other times a conference room. It's kind of the soul of

Lakshmi. It's where we all come to gather to make great things."

Jasper roped his arm around my waist and turned me toward the far wall where each of his four paintings hung side by side, each illuminated in golden amber hues of light.

"Jasper, they're stunning."

Words escaped me for just how beautiful they looked. Jasper chose to display them along a jet-black wall which was also a water feature. The paintings were set in stark relief against the glistening wall and winding vines. Almost as if the sexual deities had been caught in compromising positions in the middle of the forest.

"Won't they get wet?" I asked, touching the water as it ran down the wall.

"They're plexiglass mounted." He pointed to the closet painting and opened its plastic shell. "No moisture can get in to them. This wall is such a fantastic feature. I desperately wanted something significant enough to be able to stand up and be noticed amid this beautiful feature, but also blend. We tried oiled bronze statues, and they just felt too heavy. Plus, there's a lot of dark and we needed some color to brighten things up a bit."

"I love them."

They made me breathless. The same sensations collected low and heavy in my belly. It was as if I looked at the tawdry scenes for the first time. Seeing them again up close, especially after having now become intimate with Jasper, added a level of sensuality to them I hadn't felt before.

My nipples tightened with remembrances of the night previous. With each shift in my leggings, my thighs created enough friction to have my pussy fluttering. Jasper pulled me against his chest, his arms draped around my shoulders. The pair of us stood for long moments and just took in the beauty of his paintings. It didn't go unnoticed he was similarly affected. The hardness of his cock pressed between my cheeks, creating a volcano of desire which simmered just beneath the surface of my skin.

"I pictured you in each of these positions," he whispered in my ear. "Cradling you in Lotus, feeling your breasts pressed against mine. The two of us locked in our own cocoon of ecstasy. It's almost as appealing as spreading you open like Peasant. It's my favorite of them all. Especially imaging it's you. Your legs draped over my knees. The pinkest part of you is open and exposed for my exploration. I'd place your arms around my neck to keep them out of the way. Your pulse point in the perfect position for licking and sucking. My arm holding you by the hips so I could control our speed. You'd want to go fast because that kind of position would press right against your gspot and the moment my cock teased against your secret button, you'd be off like a prized Derby pony."

My leggings felt damp. Correction, they were beyond damp. If Jasper kept talking, I'd wantonly guide his hands beneath the waistband and greedily take what I needed from his astute surgeon's hands.

He traced the shell of my ear with his nose, breathing in the scent of me. It took every ounce of willpower to keep my legs from turning to jelly. I simultaneously tried not to wantonly press against him to greedily drink from the fountain of desire.

"Come with me, sweet Remle," he whispered, pushing my hair away from my ear. "I want to show you my hideaway."

eighteen

Jasper

Inviting Remle into my space had been a split decision. We pulled up to the distillery, and I realized I still wanted more. I wanted to learn more. To hear her laugh. See the world through her eyes. And of course, the sex was fantastic. I don't think I'd ever *not* want it with her.

I'd expected having her in my personal space after living alone for so long would feel odd, maybe even grating. All I wanted to do was lead her around and show her every square inch of my property. To show her all the ways I'd taken this broken-down thing and made it beautiful.

Somewhere in the midst of the renovations on the property—as I began outfitting it for the distillery, I discovered a little hot spring on the back of the property. I should say I discovered a *warm* spring, as most of the time it didn't get hotter than bath water. I'd brought out a landscape architect who created a little oasis for me out here. He'd carved into the pools, deep stone chairs that cradled your body while luxuriating in the heat of the sulphur spring. The clover covered path led to my private oasis was dotted with lanterns, leading up the limestone stairs to the spring.

"No one knew this was back here." I told her, helping her out of her shirt, "I stumbled upon it accidentally one day just walking the grounds. I've kept it a secret from everyone. Not even Meadow knows of its existence. I like to come here to escape the world for a little while."

I set the towels near the stairs, yanked off my T-shirt, and kicked out of my sweatpants.

I went in first, turning to gather Remle's hand in mine, and caught her openly gawking. Her eyes darkened to the color of sapphires and were full of wanton desire. She followed me into the spring, dipping her shoulders beneath the surface with a satisfied groan before taking a seat opposite me.

"This is all for you." I fisted my cock, giving it a languorous pump before taking a seat in the water.

Remle's breasts barely broke the surface of the water, teasing me every so often with a brief glimpse of her pink peaks. She leaned her head back, exposing the graceful slope of her neck, and it was like a fishhook cast into the water. I pounced on her. Needing to feel her soft skin against mine, wanting desperately to taste every centimeter of exposed skin.

I pulled the condom I discreetly tucked into the towels and ripped it open.

"Aren't you the confident one?" Remle giggled, turning in the direction of the wrapper's telltale crinkle the moment I tried to open it.

"Hopeful Remle, always hopeful for another stolen moment with you."

I exorcised the thoughts of her leaving in two days out of

my head. Thoughts of goodbyes weren't for the here and now. Right now, her lush body was naked beneath the rolling bubbles of the heated water, and I wasn't going to miss an opportunity to worship at the altar of her sensual appeal.

"Over my legs." I helped her into my lap and positioned her legs exactly as I'd fantasized. "Fuck, Remle."

She leaned back, pressing the generous globes of her ass against my groin, seeking out my cock. Her hips continued to undulate until she was able to position my cockhead at her entrance. In my mind's eye, I was the one who took control of this fantasy. The one who splayed her open and teased her clit while I made her beg for her release. Sucked her neck so hard I left a mark. Pinched at her nipples while she yelped and moaned.

I'd never imagined sitting in my lap would translate in Remle's world as sitting in the driver's seat. My cock didn't care. It was welcomed into the soft heat of Remle's pussy, with zero intentions of leaving anytime soon.

"Do you like it, sweet Remle? To be draped over my legs, on display and accessible to me?"

I traced my fingers over her outer lips, feeling the trimmed stubble tickle against the pads of my fingers. Remle's response was to open her legs wider, rock against the cock impaling her, and try to force my fingers to move a bit faster. Her inner walls strangled me. Liquid heat zinged up my spine and flooded my brain with pleasure so intense I momentarily lost sight and sound. The gentle sucking of the deepest part of Remle felt so delicious. I had to fight the urge to bite her shoulder. Instead, I flicked against her clit with my thumb as I explored where we were joined. Her delicate, silken skin stretched wide to accommodate the rod she had impaled herself on.

"Do you know why they called this position *Peasant*?" I asked, manipulating her swollen nub with focus. "it was believed only whores fucked like this. Proper women took men on their backs. Are you my whore, Remle?"

I felt her insides ripple. It took every ounce of the willpower I had to stave off the impending orgasm. I focused on how her breasts overfilled my palms. How her nipples fit perfectly in the space between my forefinger and middle finger, and how she keened every time I pinched them and tugged.

"Perhaps the question instead should be, which of us truly is the peasant? I may be in your lap spread open, but I'm also the one who controls our fate."

Her back arched to bring me as deep as I could go. The steam from the spring teased loose waves into her hair. They cascaded down her back and brushed against my face. She rocked in my lap, using the mere centimeters of space she had between my hands to push me ever closer to my finale.

"It's me." Each word she spoke came out in a rasped whisper. "I can push you over. I can let you take us over. But in this position, I'm the one driving, and our fates are tied together."

Logically, I knew she meant the fates of our orgasms. My heart, though, had different ideas. And talk of fate and tying ours together apparently was the exact trigger to push me to the point of no return.

I locked my arms around her, forced her hips down and impaled her with every millimeter of length I had left. I set a bruising pace, shoving into her as if I could put my whole body into her womb. She spread her legs wider, wrapped her arms around my neck tighter, and rode me.

I was seconds from falling over. There was absolutely no way I was going to come without her. I massaged against the area between her belly button and pelvis with each thrust into her body to stimulate her g-spot from both inside and out.

"Jasper." She held the r out on a melody of ecstasy. "Whatever you are doing, don't stop."

Those were my favorite words to hear. Instead of speeding up, I slowed down, angling my cock to try to touch my fingertips.

"Fuck."

Was there anything better than hearing a proper woman swear like the devil possessed her?

"Oh god. It's... I don't think I can hold it back." She whined, wiggling and rocking, pulling against my neck, arching toward the finger softly caressing her clit.

"When you go, I go," I told her, desperately trying to hang on to conscious thought until she did. The orgasm built with such intensity; my lips tingled. My hair follicles stood on end. Each time Remle pulled against them, they were their own island of exploding pleasure.

Words became impossible. We lifted to a plane of existence where sight, sound, and thought fell away and we lay at the altar of sensation. Each touch amplified. Every movement created a butterfly effect of electricity, winding me toward my final conclusion. I wanted to live in this place forever. Where I never wanted to stop fucking and simultaneously needed to reach the final gluttonous bite of delicious pleasure.

I felt the spasms of her release with such intensity, I'm

near certain I blacked out. One moment I cajoled her, encouraging her to let go and take us over, and the next I bounced her, hard, shoving her against my thighs, moaning myself hoarse with the vesuvian eruption that felt as if it went on for hours, though it was surely only seconds.

Shattered. Spent. Scattered. So many words to describe the particles of existence I hovered in.

"I don't think I can move." She chuckled as her body melted against mine.

"Sweet Remle. You can stay as long as you need."

Neither of us moved. I held her head tucked against my neck, her hair in a tangled mess between my fingers. I'd barely softened. I could feel blood pumping in my cock as if I hadn't come in days, despite having just finished.

One thing was certain. In a little less than a week, Remle had imbued herself into the marrow of my existence. Knowing she headed back to Lexington in just two days, words like *the future* kept coming to the forefront of my thoughts.

For the first time since I left medicine, the word fluttered with hope inside of my chest instead of drowning me in guilt.

nineteen

Reinle.

I heard a commotion somewhere close, but also far away. I couldn't make sense of it. Rather than trouble myself with whatever the noise was, I floated into consciousness, reflecting on the previous night with Jasper.

Jasper Raj. His name alone brought so many words. Passionate. Sexy. Commanding. Sweet. The things we did last night? I felt heat rise to my cheeks even in my half-awake state.

After finally finding the motivation to exit his hot spring, we ended up replicating all the positions in his paintings—throughout his house. I'd never had sex four times in one night before. Each time felt like the first time—as if we hadn't been screwing like rabbits all damn night. Even still, I felt my body stir and desire tickle through me from the mere reflection of sex with Jasper.

"Haven't I worn you out yet?"

Jasper's warm arm snaked around my hip, pulling me against the very vehicle of pleasure which kept me simultaneously ravenous and satiated concurrently. He pressed his cock between my thighs, gently scissoring in and out. He teased at my pussy, tickling and stroking everywhere but the place I needed his fingers most.

"Meadow is downstairs." Jasper nipped at my ear. "Sound carries very far in this house. Can you keep quiet, my sweet Remle?"

I showed him just how quiet I could be. I nodded, soundlessly directing his fingers to my clit, showing him exactly how hard I needed him to rub. Rather than take my direction, he scooted around me, ran his hands down my thighs before spreading me open. He took an unhurried journey, leaving sensuous kisses along my upper thighs, before kissing my pussy with the same passion as he did my mouth.

Fuck Meadow being downstairs. I did grab a pillow to try to quiet my cries as best as possible. However, Jasper's knowledge of female anatomy was so next level, every touch, caress, lick, or greedy pull from his lips against my clit left me untethered and not in control of the sounds coming out of my own mouth.

Once he added his fingers to the mix, any promise I'd made shattered into dust. I fucked greedily against those digits. Shamelessly spread wide for him. It took everything I had not to scream my completion.

"Meadow, don't try funny stuff with me. I saw his truck outside. I heard him!"

"Mrs. Raj, please. The residence is off limits. I'm trying to get Jasper on the phone. But you can't just go upstairs."

My muscles still twitched. I wasn't entirely sure I'd fully reassembled when the earlier racket became much louder and quickly approaching.

"Fuck." Jasper flew up from between my legs, and dove

next to me on the pillows, covering us both up.

"What? Who is that?"

I barely had time to get the words out of my mouth before Meadow and the tiniest sprite of a woman appeared in Jasper's bedroom.

"Mumma!" His hands shot out protectively, holding his blankets down against my naked body. Like it could possibly shield me from the abject mortification of coming face to face with his mom, two seconds after Jasper had made me come—loudly—against his tongue.

"Meadow," he barked, pointing towards the stairs with such force I heard his elbow joint crack, "get her out of here."

His mom started rattling things off in Hindi, gesticulating wildly as she did. I didn't blame her. I can only imagine how mortifying it is to see your son in bed with a woman.

"Mumma!" Jasper snapped, answering her in Hindi as well. "Go. Now. I'll be down in a minute. Meadow, please! Some assistance."

"Exactly what would you like me to do? Pull her down the stairs?"

Jasper's mom had been making her way slowly down the steps until she overheard Jasper and Meadow start to bicker. She turned around and shouted more Hindi at Jasper from her perch. If I wasn't so fucking mortified by the whole situation, I might find this whole circus comical.

"Mumma, please. Downstairs. I'm getting dressed and will be down in five minutes," he called to her. His hand was still tightly wrapped around our blankets.

"How about not letting her up here in the first damn place?" Jasper's ire boiled at full heat. Poor Meadow. It wasn't her fault. In fact, it had to be uncomfortable AF for the unfortunate woman.

"Did you not hear me tell her your residence was off limits? She's your *mom*, Jasper. It's not like she hasn't been up here before. If you're gonna have a woman here overnight, and you know, still try to run a professional business below, a courtesy text might have been smart."

"Meadow, I swear to god. Tread lightly right now. You can return downstairs. Please make her a cup of tea. She prefers the Massala Chai. There's a box in the test kitchen, to the right of the sink."

I could see a retort forming on Meadow's lips, but thankfully she thought better of giving it a voice. Instead, she turned and shot down the stairs at a jog. Seconds later, you could hear her clanging what felt like every pot known to man in the test kitchen.

"This was not the kind of wake up I'd been hoping for today." Jasper ran his hand down my face, cradling my jaw. "I'm sorry to have exposed you to something embarrassing."

"I think you were a bit hard on Meadow. If it weren't for her playing defense, your mom would have seen quite a show had she arrived even two minutes earlier."

That got a laugh out of him.

"You're so damn perfect." He kissed me, long and slow. As if he didn't have an impatient mom sipping Masala Chai downstairs, counting the seconds until his arrival. The muscles in his face relaxed just slightly, though the deep frown lines above his eyes stayed where they were.

"Take your time up here. I have no idea why my mom is here or what she wants. Don't feel pressured to do anything you don't want. If you want to take a shower, have some breakfast, hang out and watch TV while I sort her out, you're totally welcome to. If you want to come down and join me, you can do that too."

Jasper pushed out of bed, his still half hard cock bouncing against his thigh as he dug through his drawers for a pair of sweatpants.

"This is definitely not how I planned to spend today." He sighed, yanking on a T-shirt. "I feel bad." He leaned over the bed, guiding me toward his mouth with his fingertips on my chin. "I promise I'll make this up to you."

Once Jasper went downstairs, I took my time putzing around and getting my day started. I had a few emails I replied to, handled a few last-minute requests for information on the upcoming Bourbon Appreciation Day from my cell phone, and spent far too long in Jasper's shower. Which was luxe with a capital L. I had to convince myself three separate times I was for real getting out of the shower before I actually did. All of those jets.

"You brought me bio-data?"

The voices downstairs had been a quiet murmur. I'd practically forgotten Jasper's mom and he were downstairs. Until I could practically see his shout reverberating against the pitched beams of his loft.

"... so many good matches in North Carolina... good schools... tech boom... great families."

I didn't hear their entire conversation, but I got enough pieces to suss out why she was here.

"I'm not interested." I heard a clatter of plates and

assumed someone was washing dishes.

"Because of the one upstairs?" I heard, clearly. "Two days ago, you told me you're too busy to find good women. So I come here. I bring Mahadeva with me so she can find you a good wife. This way, you can still do your business, and we can help you."

"Mumma, I am married to my *job*. I don't want bio-data because I don't want a wife. I'm sorry you flew all of this way, but please—this is the worst possible time for me to have visitors. I have to bottle this weekend."

There was absolutely no reason I should feel a pang in my chest. I'd started this dalliance with Jasper with eyes wide open. But I guess somewhere between our first kiss and now I felt like the near transcendent sex, being welcomed into the warm embrace of his friend group, and overall *really* liking being in his company—we'd figure out a way to be a long distance couple.

"But this one upstairs, you have time for her? Is she even from a good family? What do you know about her?"

"Her name is Remle, Mumma. And I'm not discussing this with you."

The two of them started bickering in Hindi again. Rather than hide up here and play voyeur to their disagreement— and similarly, I didn't need to bear witness to her insults. I grabbed my bag and my cell phone and went down the main stairs, away from where they sat in the test kitchen.

Meadow watched me walk out but didn't say anything —not even a passing *have a nice day*. Whether it was to protect my quiet exit, or because she harbored some kind of ill will toward me because Jasper snapped at her—I didn't bother to stop and discuss. I guessed I was going back to Lexington empty handed.

twenty

Jasper

H onestly, what the fuck. Usually, I'd be over the moon, thrilled my mom came to visit. But this? With her friend's damn nayan in tow? This could not be my life. Of all the things I didn't have time for right now, this shit sat at the top of my list.

Both of my parents recently retired. Meera and I left the nest in a big way. We both lived on opposite sides of the country. I'm sure my mom was a little bored without her work to monopolize all her waking hours. Her friends had children who didn't spend ten years of their lives in school and started families much sooner than Meera and I. Now her sole focus was to obsess over us day and night. I couldn't wait to break away from this ridiculous conversation, go and check on poor mortified Remle, and send an SOS to my sister.

"J.R., I'm sorry to interrupt time with your Mom, but Gemini is on the phone and needs to talk to you. She says it's urgent."

We literally just left. What could possibly be wrong already?

"Gemini, what's the matter?"

"Oh thank god. I tried calling your cell like fifteen times. What the fuck happened with Remle?"

My brain couldn't catch up to her words fast enough. Having my mother seated in the tasting room with Mahadeva drinking their tea, eating their cookies, and still mulishly flipping through her binder full of women, I had zero interest in meeting.

"Okay, I admit, meeting your boyfriend's mother two seconds after having a very loud orgasm is probably a totally mortifying experience. I honestly don't think my mom even realized we'd *literally* just finished having sex. We were just, you know, naked—together—in my bed. To be honest, my mom is more concerned with having grandbabies, so the sex part is probably a good sign for her."

The line was so quiet I thought we'd gotten disconnected.

"Gem?"

"Jasper, when's the last time you talked to Remle?"

I looked at my watch. Jesus, it was already going on lunch time. The poor thing had been hiding in my house for over four hours.

"I think around eight-ish. Honestly, I was so shocked my mother was standing at the foot of my bed. I don't even know what time it was she showed up."

"Where exactly do you think Remle is, Jasper?"

"Gemmy, to be honest, today has been a complete shitshow. My mom is here, and she brought a friend to act as my matchmaker. She walked in on Remle and I having sex, and I've spent hours going around in circles with my mother about arranged marriages and the kind of wife my mother thinks I need. Please spare me the guessing games. What is it you need? Do you need me to go and get Remle?"

The phones in the distillery were all wireless and linked to an entire hyper complicated system allowing us to hand off calls from one office or building to another. I took the stairs up to my residence two at a time, expecting to see Remle lazing on my couch in front of my oversized TV. She wasn't in my bedroom, or the bathroom either.

"That's weird. She's not up here." I said it more to myself than to Gemini.

"Jesus Jasper, I've been trying to tell you. She went home. She's probably nearly there by now."

"What did she say when you talked to her?" I asked, jogging down the staircase and toward the front doors where Meadow sat. Surely, she would have had to see her leave.

"I didn't say much. She was crying so hard I was really scared she was going to drive off the road."

Gemini had no idea the weight those words had. How deeply enmeshed in my psyche they were. The reaction to them was instantaneous. No longer was I looking at the oversized black slate doors with the ornate lotus flowers cut in stained glass. I stood in a room which smelled of antiseptic and the cloying, coppery scent of blood. I heard the flatline. The nurse told me to call it. I looked at the time, three oh seven, twenty-one. We shouted for the recovery team. Made the thoracic cut, separated the breast bone to massage the heart until they arrived. *Dr. Raj, no!* She said, *Her hand. Dr. Raj, her hand. It's moving. Dr. Raj!*

"Jasper?" Meadow's cold hands swept against my face. "J.R. please, you're the doctor, not me. I'm sorry I called you a stupid prick. Just wake the fuck up because your mom is freaking out and shouting at me in another language and I don't know what to do."

"You gave us all quite a shock." My mom sat next to me on the sofa, holding a cold compress to my head.

With Gavin's help—Meadow called him—I made it upstairs to my living room sofa. I hadn't had a panic attack that severe in at least two years. It was well after dinner time and Meadow still flittered around, ordering take out, making sure my mom was okay. I saw her in my periphery, putting two cups of tea and some scones on the coffee table.

"Thank you, Meadow." The muscles in my mouth felt sluggish and off. I think I gave her at least a halfhearted smile. "I really appreciate all the help."

"I didn't know you two were arguing," she said. "When Remle left, I just assumed the two of you had—you know— had a game plan when you came down to greet your mom. If I had known, I could have at least asked her what her plans were."

"It's fine, Meadow. I really do appreciate you stuck around and help with my mom. I probably don't say thank you as much as I should."

Her lip quivered. The stony, sometimes prickly, always reliable, Meadow, was getting choked up.

"I'm sorry I snapped at you earlier. Tomorrow, lattes and scones on me."

Meadow nodded, waved, and skipped down the stairs. I assumed to head out for the evening.

"This has happened before?" my mom asked, pulling my focus back. The pitch of her voice said she already knew the answer. I nodded, unable to say the words.

"This is why you left medicine?"

"Part of the reason," I admitted, sitting up and trying to rub the remaining haze away. "After what happened, I couldn't stay. My reputation was too far damaged. And I just didn't have it in me anymore."

"You look different." Her fingers tickled through my hair as she adjusted it in a direction which suited her. "You've finally got some meat on your bones. I noticed you've eaten through almost all the food I cooked for you. Mahadeva and I will go to the store tomorrow, and we'll make you more."

She nodded as if we'd actually been discussing it, and she won the final say. I was far too exhausted to have an opinion. Except I needed to call Remle.

"You're happy. I can see it in your face." Her hands were cool and smelled like the lemon hand lotion she'd kept in her purse since we were kids. "This place, your business, you seem at peace here."

"I am, Mumma. I built Lakshmi from a single bourbon bottle. And now it's about to get really big. Bigger than I ever expected it to be. For the first time I can see a *future* Mumma, and not just a list of my responsibilities between today and tomorrow or the next thing to achieve. I can see all the possibilities in front of me and I'm *excited*. I want you to be excited, too."

"I worry you are here alone with no one to take care of you. A good wife—"

"Mumma, please. A wife will come when I'm ready, not from Mahadeva's bio-data binders and you pressuring me to take time away from the things I love to have drinks and forced conversations with people I couldn't care less about."

"Is this because of the redhead? The one who doesn't know how to keep quiet when company is around?"

For being so tiny, my mom had quite a sassy attitude, and gave zero fucks who did or didn't want to hear her opinions.

"Her name is Remle. And we didn't know we had company. You'd think someone would call and give us the heads up."

She threw her hands up in the air as if to say, oh well.

"Where is she? Remle?"

I pushed myself to standing and searched around for my cell phone. I had about a million missed called from Gemini and a few random text messages from some of the guys, but nothing from the only person I wanted to hear from.

"I think you spooked her," I answered honestly. "All your talk of bio-data and finding me a wife probably made her feel like she wasn't good enough."

Me: Gem, has Remle made it home safe? I had an emergency and am just now getting back to you. I'm sorry our conversation got cut short earlier.

Gemini: She's home.

Gemini: You're on my shit list, Jasper Raj.

Gemini: She sounded so fucking sad.

Gemini: You need to fix this.
Me: I promise, it's just a misunderstanding.

"Does she have nice, wide hips?" my mother asked. "Good hips mean healthy babies."

twenty-one

Remle.

Being home brought me zero joy. The townhouse I'd rented since getting my job with the Bourbon Association had always been a point of pride. It was a nice home, and I did it on my own. I didn't need anyone to help me with the deposit or buying furniture. Nothing.

I'd spoken to Gemini on my way home—and then a three-way call between me, Gemini, and Amelia—and unpacked the whole week for them. I'd hoped they'd tell me I was over-reacting. I was reading far more into our little hookup than was necessary. Instead, I could feel their empathy over the speakers in my car and I lost it.

Gemini had been flat out shocked we'd only known each other a week. According to her, we had "off the charts chemistry." So much for her assertion.

"Earth to Clay." Shep sauntered into my office and perched on the corner of my desk.

Sleep evaded me. I never heard from Jasper. Not by nine o'clock when I decided there was no point pretending to be interested in whatever played on my television. Not at eleven when I got up to get some water and use the bathroom. Not at one thirty when I couldn't sleep and stared endlessly at the celling wondering what to do. And even at five thirty, when I woke up to start getting ready for work, I still hadn't heard a thing from him.

It began to feel like I'd imagined the whole silly relationship. But even Gemini said she felt a connection. The sex had been incredible. I didn't think you could have transformative sex without some emotion tied to it. Maybe it was just me.

"Give me the download on Raj."

He was funny. And loved his friends. His lips were so undeniably kissable. His cock? Other worldly. He was smart and ambitious, but also humble. So many things I wanted to say, but none of them were what Shep cared about.

"There isn't much to offer you, Shep. Lakshmi, without a doubt, will be one of the most successful single batch distributors. But they still have copies of their rejection letter. It's not something they're going to just forgive and forget, Shep. The last board really damaged relationships with so many distillers who would have made amazing members of our board and community."

He waved a piece of paper before placing it in front of me.

"Well, you convinced them somehow. Their lawyers just sent this over."

He did it. Signed my contract. Joined the association at a much higher level than was necessary, but he was all in for full promotion. He wanted the Bourbon Trail, publicity consultation, the whole nine yards.

"I'll get a press release ready to announce it."

Shep high-fived me, showering me in praise. I smiled at

him, but it was empty. I felt nothing. I should be proud, feel some sense of accomplishment. But the contract didn't feel like a win. It felt like a consolation prize.

"Press release? Oh no. This is big. I'm sending you back down there for Bourbon Appreciation Day next week. We need full court on this. Get all the local press in North Carolina on the story. I want headlines, Remle." He pointed to the air above his head, spreading his hands out as if smoothing out an old school newspaper he probably had never experienced reading. "Like a good neighbor... Bourbon Association extends trail into North Carolina."

"But—you're taking over as the account manager, right?"

"Why would I do that?"

He took a seat in the chair across from my desk and folded his arms across his chest. He was dressed in the most obnoxious seersucker suit with a polka-dot bow tie. I barely had combined four hours of good sleep. Dealing with the present assault to the eyes he wore, I needed him out of my office.

"Because clients are your responsibility, not mine."

"Except this is *your* client. You got the contract signed. I thought you'd be thrilled to have the opportunity to personally handle Lakshmi."

"That's not me, Shep. I'm not a salesperson."

"Remle, there's nothing to sell. It's an account all you need to do is manage it."

I pushed against my eyes. I'm certain the move smeared all of my eye makeup, but I ceased caring. Jasper had made it clear from his lack of communication he wasn't interested in continuing whatever we'd started. I'd be okay with it. Eventually I'd get over it, but not before I would need to drive *back* to North Carolina and spend days setting up press junkets and whatever the hell else Shep envisioned.

"Shep, this is *your* job, not mine. Now, I'm going to contact Mr. Raj and do a soft handoff, and then I wash my hands of the account entirely."

twenty-two

Gemini refused to give me Remle's cell phone number. The personal one. Not the one on her business cards which went to voice mail. She said when Remle was ready to talk to me, she would. I should give her the space to process. I had zero clue what Gemini meant by it.

I'd intended to join the Bourbon Association anyway. I'd made the decision somewhere around the time Remle convinced the whole town we needed a spot on the Bourbon Trail for consistent tourism. Her kind of moxie turned me the hell on. I respected her for researching enough to know what the town needed and discovering a way her product could meet the need.

Was it desperate to send the contract first thing in the morning because I couldn't get a hold of my girlfriend after a misunderstanding? Sure. Perhaps calling her my girlfriend was a bit premature, given we hadn't even discussed it. It seemed silly to call her anything but though. In just a few days, she'd insinuated herself so deep into my existence I couldn't imagine not having her around.

"Remle, I've been so worried."

I answered on the first ring. If it hadn't specifically said Bourbon Association on the caller I.D. the 859 area code would have been giveaway.

"Mr. Raj, good morning. This is Remle Clay from the National Bourbon Association."

"Remle, sweetheart. I know it's you. Listen I'm so sorry about my mom. I know it was the worst situation to wake up to, and I'll make it up to you. I just—I need you to come back so we can talk about this face to face.

"I first wanted to thank you so much for joining our humble association. I know you will be so thrilled with all of the ancillary ways a membership with the NBA provides value to all of your customers."

Her voice held zero warmth. It was as if she read from a notepad. With each sentence, my anxiety twisted higher. This wasn't the Remle I wanted. I needed to talk to the real Remle. Even if she bawled me out for not coming to check on her sooner. Or not standing up to my mom fast enough. Or listed any number of things I did wrong.

"Rem...this isn't you. Please can you drop the act and just talk to me. I have so much to say I'm sorry for. But I want to say it to the real you, not a robot."

"It was so great working with you this past week and learning all about Lakshmi. But, it's time I pass you along to our Senior Director of Accounts, Shepard Estes. He will make sure anything you need gets taken care of."

I didn't want him. I wanted Remle, in all ways obviously, but in this instance, I wanted her mind, her creativity, the way she looked at problems and found solutions. The truth was I needed her.

"Remle Clay—damnit! Talk to me. Please?"

"Again, it was so nice meeting you and learning about Lakshmi. You are doing great things down there, and I for one am so excited to see where they go. Shep is right here, so I'm going to turn the call over to him. Best of luck, Mr. Raj."

"Remle! Wait! Please!"

I felt sick. My heart beat so hard my Apple Watch flashed warning signs at me. I couldn't stop and take a breath, not until I figured out what the fuck was going on with Remle.

"Mr. Raj, Shepard Estes. I want to thank you again for your—"

"Shepard, Remle and I were in the middle of a very important product campaign when she felt obligated to return because of your incessant pestering for a signed contract. You have my signature. Now, I need something from you. I don't care if you need to hog tie her into the back of whatever lifted truck you've convinced yourself you needed and drag her ass back to North Carolina, but I expect you and she to be down here by midday tomorrow. No excuses."

"Mr. Raj, Ms. Clay has requested to be reassigned. I'm not certain I can guarantee your request."

"I suggest you find a way to guarantee it. I have a letter here stating you aren't interested in partnering with my little distillery. How would that read up on social media? Tomorrow, by one o'clock, Shep. Don't let me down."

Mind you, the stupid letter didn't mean shit to me. I hadn't joined NBA because I cared about esteem. I joined because Remle's ideas were worth more than their stupid annual fees, and the town was right—we really could benefit from the additional tourism. Sycamore Mountain saved me when I thought I had nothing left to give. It was time for me to return the favor.

It turned out Shep couldn't perform miracles. There was a lot of red tape he needed to navigate with his company. Which wasn't detrimental, and not really a surprise. Companies had rules, I could respect that. It didn't mean I wasn't impatient. He promised me they would be down in time for Bourbon Appreciation Day, as they wanted to use the opportunity to announce their expansion into North Carolina. Fine. I could wait four days.

twenty-three

Remle.

Shep: I'll drive to NC. I can't play passenger for five hours in your clown car.

Not everyone could afford a BMW SUV. Regardless though, was he high? I didn't want to go back down there. And I especially didn't want to road trip with him.

Remle: Lakshmi is your client, what do you need me for?

I saw the ellipses showing he was responding, hang there for a good twenty seconds and then disappear.

"You are the head of Public Relations and promotions are you not?"

Shep stood at my door in another one of his over-styled suits. I nodded. I knew what he would say before the words were even out of his mouth. I already knew I wasn't going to like it.

"They may be my account now, but it's your

responsibility to promote them. You're coming down to get the press junket handled, to work with the local businesses to let them know what to expect in the coming months—do I really need to tell you how to do your job?"

He didn't. I knew all of this. The thought of seeing Jasper face to face had my insides twisting.

"Whatever happened last week—I don't want to know. I get it, you don't want to see Mr. Raj."

I tried to object but he held his hand up to stop me before I started talking.

"No need to give me an explanation. It's not my business. But like it or not getting Lakshmi on the Bourbon Trail is a big deal. And whether you want to think it is or not —it's because of you, Remle. So, I say this with so much respect and admiration—but put your big girl panties on, suck it up, and handle your shit."

Shep was not nearly as fun to ride in a car with than Jasper had been. At least Jasper let me pick what radio station to listen to. Shep listened to sports talk radio obsessively and I was about to poke out my ear drums.

"I'm famished," Shep said as we pulled into Sycamore Mountain.

He was all about efficiency, therefore the only stop we'd made since leaving Lexington were for bathroom breaks and to fill up one time for gas. He'd picked me up equipped with green smoothies and protein bars for the ride down—no thank you. I took it as a clear sign he would be completely averse to road trip snacks. No junk food, check. The stop at the gas station hadn't done anything but poke at the festering wound named Jasper Raj.

"Can we go and check in first before we go and eat lunch?"

I didn't really want to eat lunch with him. I'd be perfectly fine checking in to the White Oak, saying hi to Iris, and just ordering something to deliver.

"Nonsense. There's a diner right here."

He pulled into Wallflower and cut the engine.

"Remle! Oh my gosh, I didn't know if I'd ever see you again. You cut out of here so fast!" Briar greeted us at the door, enthusiastically chatting as she led us to a booth near the back. "Who's your friend?"

She tossed her pink tipped hair and adjusted her glasses, gracing Shep with a smile so sweet I was tempted to check my glucose levels.

"This is my boss, Shepard Estes."

"Call me Shep," he said, returning her smile, "Everyone does."

After what seemed like an endless stare off between the two of them, Briar finally snapped out of whatever haze she'd been in.

"I almost forgot! I have something for you." She dashed to her counter and returned before I could even question what on earth she could possibly have for me.

As soon as I saw the envelope with the elegant scribble of my name, I knew.

Remle,
If it weren't for you coming to Wallflower and chatting it up with
Iris's crafting circle—I don't know if this crazy brilliant idea of
yours would have ever taken flight. I never told you how
impressed I was (and still am) you listened, heard, and came up
with a solution
which benefitted the greater good.
It's one of the many traits of yours
which are so incredibly attractive to me.
Jasper

I could barely breathe, let alone compute a sentence properly. What on earth was Jasper playing at? How on earth did he know I'd come to Wallflower, anyway? I answered the question in a nanosecond given there weren't very many establishments in Sycamore Mountain it was safe to assume I'd be here at some point.

"What's that?"

Shep interrupted my musings.

"Nothing. Just a letter from one of the locals complimenting me on getting the Bourbon Trail out here."

"All right let's get checked in and then we can have a little confab about all the shit we still need to get done."

He threw a fifty-dollar bill on the table, winked at Briar, and we headed to his car.

"My star! I am so glad to see you again!" Iris had me choked in super aggressive hug the moment I stepped over the threshold. "I can't believe you pulled it off, sugar! I tell you, we're all a bunch of bees in pollen. You just tell me what you need, and I will get everyone to fall in line!" It was then she noticed Shep, "Is this your boyfriend?"

Iris asked, the shock in her voice totally apparent. I guess she was old school southern. The kind who thought gorgeous, model-esque men only belonged with gorgeous model-esque women.

"This is Shepard Estes, my boss at the Bourbon Association."

"Oh, of course. Well Mr. Estes, you have a great one. Probably the best. I'm sure you hear it every day, but this young lady is deserving of every word of praise in the dictionary."

She handed us our key cards and pointed Shep in the direction of his room.

"Just let me set my bags down, and I'll come back so we can talk about what needs to be done for the press junket, okay?"

Iris saluted me with a wink and a smile.

Sitting on the desk in my room was a gigantic basket. Not just any gigantic basket, but a basket from Honey Bunz, wrapped in their adorable bee ribbons and chock full of scones and other goodies. Inside was another note with the same elegant scribble.

Remle,
I promise I had no idea you were staying here. I should have never given your basket away.
If I had known then what I know now, I would have cherished every opportunity to get to know you better, including keeping the basket
and inviting you over to share it with me.

You have a well of kindness which never runs dry.
Another one of your many traits
that are so incredibly attractive.
Jasper

Two notes? I didn't know Jasper's endgame. My phone was in my hand about to call, when Shep knocked on my door.

"Rem, we've gotta get some of these things knocked out. I just got a call from WBWN and they need logistics sent over for the news van."

I grabbed my purse & laptop and followed him to the reception area.

"All right, Iris has troops assembling here in about twenty minutes. They'll help me canvas the local businesses with the flyers and signs announcing the partnership and promote the new stop on the trail. You should probably head to Lakshmi and figure out where Jasper wants the press to congregate. FaceTime me when you've got the info and then I can coordinate with the news outlets."

He swung his keys around his finger with a wink and pushed through the front door.

"Remle! Child, I think you need to go on a televangelist tour, because you have the gift!" Aiden rushed straight to me the moment he spotted me. "Do you know Jasper and I had an actual conversation yesterday? He came in and asked me to make that basket for you, and we *talked*. A full-fledged conversation, Remle! One which had a salutation, some stuff in-between and a valediction."

"Valediction?" Addison laughed and slapped him on the

chest. "Don't choke on big words. It was literally a three-minute conversation."

"Yes, but it was a conversation."

Iris cleared her throat and waived me over to where she stood with the members of her crafting group. She must have put out a significant S.O.S. There were at least a hundred people who had come to help.

twenty-four

Jasper

Shepard Estes was exactly as I expected him to be. Decked out in head-to-toe Vineyard Vines, pulling up in a jet black BMW SUV, using "yessir" like he got paid for it—my patience began to unravel.

"Again sir, I want to extend my sincere apologies for the letter. The previous board wanted to protect a legacy of distilling which had modernized and changed—"

I didn't care. Every word he said was a drumbeat of *Remle, Remle*. I knew she was nearby. Iris told me two rooms were booked for the NBA for the same length of time.

"Where do you advise having this junket?" I asked.

"We can have it wherever you think would be best to host a large crowd. Maybe here in the tasting room?"

"This only seats twenty, and even with people standing we wouldn't be able to get more than say thirty in here."

He stood too close to me, with his hands on his hips surveying the room.

"We could always take the table and chairs out."

"The table was crafted from an actual fallen tree. It weighs hundreds of pounds."

Meadow came up alongside me with the office phone. The moment I saw it, my heart actually skipped it's beat. I thought Remle was calling to tell me she'd seen the basket and wanted to talk.

"The crew needs to speak with you," she said, pressing the phone into my hand.

It was our code when she thought I needed an out because I looked uncomfortable.

"I'll get Remle on the phone." Shep offered, "I'll have her offer her thoughts while you're dealing with the crew."

I didn't want to leave. I wanted to hear her voice, see her face. It had been less than a week, but something deep inside pushed me to stay to make sure she was okay.

Meadow and I stepped just outside the tasting area so I could hold a pretend conversation with my crew.

"Briar texted to tell me those two are at lunch there before checking into the hotel."

So, she had two of my notes then. Fantastic. I hoped she'd be able to collect all of them before she arrived at the distillery tomorrow. It would make trying to apologize to her so much easier if she heard from me how much I adored her.

"Have you spoken to Jasper?" I heard her ask Shep. She sounded tired. Or maybe sad. I didn't know her well enough to know what the pitch of her voices sounded like for different emotions, but I knew it definitely didn't sound like the Remle I'd interacted with for four days.

"Please tell her I know she has a vision for this, and she has full access to whatever her vision entails." I told him over my pretend phone call.

"Did you hear that?" Shep asked.

She must have signaled understanding somehow. I desperately wanted to know where she was. I wanted to go to her. To apologize, or explain, and let her know just how much I valued the person she was. But I needed to be patient and stick with my plan. Soon enough, I hoped, she'd be back.

twenty-five

Remle

There wasn't a single business in Sycamore Mountain that didn't have Bourbon Trail signs in their windows, pamphlets detailing what it was, information on the benefits of collecting stamps in the Bourbon Trail passport, and a rundown on talking points. The excitement surrounding our involvement was as palpable as a heartbeat.

"Last on your list I see." Ian laughed while accepting my goodie bag.

"Only because I wanted to give myself some time to linger and say hello."

Ian directed me toward the same booth I'd sat in the week prior, while he whipped me up a latte.

"Ms. Clay, you are pure magic. Benefits to the town aside, what kind of spell have you cast on our town misanthrope?"

I must have made some kind of confused face because Ian nearly startled me out of my skin with his belly laugh.

"He came in here yesterday afternoon. Had a beer. Sat

right over there at the bar." He pointed over his shoulder to where he'd just been making my coffee. "Sang like a songbird about Dr. Zane, his life in Chicago, the day he moved here and how much he appreciated both my kindness and my discretion. Then he poured his heart out to *me* of all people! A gay man in a small town who has zero game and no advice to offer when it comes to women. Yet I'm the one he decides to unburden himself about a woman who just danced into his life and shook him right up. Made him see things differently. Directed his chin from looking back and showed him how to look up and enjoy the view once in a while."

I didn't want those words to insinuate themselves into my heart. They weren't welcome. They were just words. Empty words which meant nothing.

"Except I'm neither Indian, nor thin—so" I shrugged, "why invest in something when it won't go anywhere?"

I should have kept my mouth shut. There were so many tiny details I still needed to tend to, and I couldn't get sidetracked by my emotions. The truth was I *wanted* to think about *more* with Jasper. Not right away. But I want to walk a path with someone I could see a potential future with.

"It sounds like a deeper conversation than one to have with me, but from what I saw I think you are incorrect."

"His mom blatantly said she wanted him to marry someone from this binder she brought. Someone Indian. Someone from a good family. Someone intelligent and successful so they could make perfect babies together. At this point in my life, I don't want to date someone temporary. I don't want a partner for a good time who will eventually tell me they want to settle down with someone and not just *coast* with me anymore."

Ian didn't need to know my backstory. He had other things to worry about than Remle Clay and the college boyfriend she'd spent nearly all of her twenties with. How she'd waited for the proposal to come, only for him to tell her he couldn't see a future with her.

Ian pulled a letter from his back pocket. The same handwriting as the other two. This one in an actual envelope instead of just folded into itself.

Remle,

I stood across the street, watching you smile and chat with Ian. You went in there, intent to learn anything you could about the town, bourbon distilling, flavor profiles, all so you could come to me well armed with ideas to help shepherd my success in new directions.

I watched you from across the street. I desperately wanted to learn more about you but was unsure exactly how to approach you. It had been too long since I'd dated anyone. So long since I'd had anyone experience life so close to me.

You charged across the street, dragging that sunshine you notoriously carry on a chain, and pushed into my space. Looked at those paintings alongside me, and every moment you stood there I couldn't stop thinking about all the ways you tied me up inside. And of course...all the ways I could re-enact those paintings that hung on the wall.

You are a goddess. One I want to get to know more. I admire your wit, your charm, and how effortless it is for you to make friends with absolutely everyone.

You are so beautiful. You're beautiful in your summer dresses, in your power suits with your lips painted in colors that make me think dirty thoughts. You're beautiful in borrowed sundresses, and also ratty old college t-shirts that show your nipples (I'm not complaining, I will always appreciate that view and insist you wear your shirt to bed until it falls off your body).

Our last night together is on never-ending repeat. I want all of it, again, many times in a day. The other thing I can't stop replaying in my head is the last time I saw you. How euphoric we were. How I couldn't get enough of you. I planned to spend the whole day lazing away in bed making a mental road map of every single thing that brought you pleasure.

I'm so sorry we got interrupted. And most of all, I'm sorry any conversation I had with my mom led you to believe in any way you aren't good enough.

It is the furthest thing from the truth.

My mom's arrival was a collection of worries on her part. I was wasting away here, listlessly existing with no purpose. She thought she'd be coming and seeing the same person who left Chicago seven years ago. It isn't the case. Especially not since I met you, and she saw it. How fulfilling Lakshmi has been for me, and how you've helped me to find new directions to take it to build a future overflowing with possibility.

I told her ever since meeting you I feel like I can see a future. I can look ahead instead of always looking back. I don't want to lose it. I don't want to lose you. You brought the sun, Remle Clay, and I want to explore what a life of sunshine looks like with you.

Love,

Jasper

Wow. I had no words. It seemed as if Ian could sense it. He left the table and allowed me the space of my own thoughts.

160

twenty-six

I felt like I was in junior high all over again, asking my friends if they'd passed my note in study hall. I thought for sure I'd have heard from Remle by now. I only had so much patience for Shep when the only person I wanted to ask questions of and discuss strategy with was nowhere to be found.

"Have you heard from Remle?" I asked as Shep started packing up and talking about plans for the morning.

"No it's been a while since we've touched base. She was going to meet with the local businesses and then with all of the T.V. stations. I'm going to head back to the Inn, would you like to come with?"

I wanted to. I refrained. I'd see her in the morning, even if the whole night would be pure torture.

I'd lived alone in my house since I purchased it. Sure the crew was here during bottling and distribution. But it was mine, alone. It never bothered me. In fact, the solitude had always been something I'd not only enjoyed but craved.

When Shep left, the house felt *too* quiet. Lonely. For the

first time since moving in, the last place I wanted to be was there, by myself.

Rather than spend time moping in the residence, or obsessing over tiny details, I walked the path to the hot spring hoping the heat would both soothe and relax me.

"Did you really mean all of this?"

I hadn't had a single thing to drink other than water all day. I knew I wasn't drunk. I'd slept a full eight hours the night previous, so I wasn't hallucinating. Remle sat on the rocks, her toes skimming the water, my letter between her hands. She had to have read it a few times—I could see the visible creases of being folded over and again.

"Every word," I said, taking a seat next to her. "I've never met anyone like you, Remle. Since meeting you, I feel —awake."

"Jasper." The way she said my name imbued me with hope. One word held so much meaning. "I'm sorry I just left. I should have stayed. Should have let you explain. I just— I've felt the sting of rejection so many times having to face the truth with someone whom I truly felt something—it hurt. And I couldn't figure out why after only knowing you for such a short time I would feel an emotion so strongly, but I think it's because I'm falling in love with you."

She turned and faced me, her bottom lip tucked beneath her teeth, a crooked, unsure smile trying to break free from between the confines of those teeth.

I know it seems way too soon, but I feel like sometimes you just know."

I did know. I knew it all too well in fact. Mainly because fighting with my mom over something I categorically *didn't* want, showed me in the most crystalline way, everything I did. And that was a future with Remle Clay.

"It's a good thing I've already fallen then," I pulled her in and kissed her, "because I'm waiting, ready to catch you."

Bourbon Appreciation Day was a whirlwind of activity I never expected but simultaneously am so grateful to Remle for organizing. She and Shep must have called every television station in a five-county area and told them to come under threat of something. Our demonstration room was packed to the gills with tv crews, residents of Sycamore Mountain, and a few well knowns, to my surprise, like Chef Tobin Laurent and Gemini Tate.

Seeing Tobin was a huge shock. I would have never expected him to find time out of his insane schedule to fly across the country, but Remle had begged him to come to help drum up more interest for the television crews. She'd also somehow convinced my sister to come, who also got the word to my parents it was an important step for Lakshmi. Everyone I loved all came to bear witness to the new chapter of Lakshmi.

Beneath the paintings which inspired the new line, Remle and I rolled out Kama Sutra, our affordable, single year bottles at the forty-dollar price point. Her instincts had been spot on. No sooner had I announced the new label, it was sold out in twenty minutes. We were going to have to expand to keep up with the dual demands of both labels.

"Ms. Clay, I have to say you are a miracle worker."

We sat at the banquet tables the town helped set up in the distilling barn. The amount of effort and work that went in to creating this sort of after event celebration boggled my mind. I was no one in the grand scheme of things. A no one who never even had the courtesy to have conversations with most of these people. Yet, a week with Remle Clay, and they all rolled out the welcome mat and did their level best to create this magical moment.

"It's nothing more than everything you deserve."

Her joy was like tasting the first cold sip of fresh spring water as winter melted away. I wanted to gluttonously drink from the fountain every single day. Though, as much as I purged on her light, I knew logically, we had some coordination to work out in the near future.

"Thank you for all of this, Remle Clay. I don't know what I did to deserve someone like you waltzing into my life—but I will be grateful every day you did."

epilogue

Remie.

What a difference a year makes. Working with Jasper and the Lakshmi brand had taught me a lot about myself, professionally. Relationship with Jasper aside, I realized I'd been coasting for way too long. Whether it was because Holt dying changed my perspective on wanting to stay close to home, or having a boyfriend tell you he wasn't interested in marrying you—somewhere along the lines I lost myself and just got comfortable existing, and doing life the easy way.

Going toe to toe with Jasper Raj and Meadow had shown me I had a whole host of skills in my toolbox I had forgotten about. I spent so many years doing the same things on repeat, I forgot how fun a challenge could be. And finding solutions to problems? What a high! Especially when those solutions began to pay off in triplicate.

Jasper and I do the long-distance thing. We drive back and forth between Lexington and Sycamore Mountain at least twice a month. And, professionally, I have been advising him on the launch of Kama Sutra Bourbon, whose first batch will be ready for sampling for Lakshmi's inaugural year on the Bourbon Trail.

The year also helped me to realize how much I love Public Relations. Not only in regard to Lakshmi and Kama Sutra, but also advising Gemini on her medical clinic. Success with that expanded into a paid gig for their restaurant The Tuckaway Tavern, and now I have new requests for consulting work at least once a week. I'm about to take the scariest step of my life and leave the Bourbon Association.

Jasper, my favorite cheerleader, has been encouraging from the sidelines every step of the way. He showed me how satisfying pursuing passions can be. In fact, I'll be hanging the sign for Remle Clay Consulting—with an eventual better name, from Sycamore Mountain.

"I can't believe this turnout!"

Jasper and I walked toward the distillery to celebrate the official tasting of Kama Sutra's first batch—in coordination with the Bourbon Appreciation celebrations. Nearly all of Jasper's family and our friends showed up once again for the occasion. Even my parents had come to support Jasper, with my little niece in tow.

"I want to thank everyone who is here for your support. The town of Sycamore Mountain, you all have wrapped your arms around me and ingratiated me into this town. I am so grateful to each of you, and regret it took me so long to finally become a true Sycamore Mountain resident."

He truly had become one with Sycamore Mountain. He'd even been convinced by the principal of the high school to allow them to use his barn for the Sadie Hawkins dance last fall. Apparently it was now going to be an annual tradition.

"I know you are all here for an official tasting of the new

Kama Sutra line, but before we uncork the batch, I'd like to show you all something extra special."

Jasper turned to the table behind him and grabbed the most exquisite bottle. It was dark red, with Sanskrit writing all over the bottle in vibrant pink, blue, and orange.

"This bottle is a gift to the one woman who has shown me how to truly find pleasure in every step of my life's journey. A few weeks ago I put a special recipe exclusive to this batch, in its barrel, and stored it deep in our coiffeurs with a date twenty five years in the future as it's intended bottle date. It will be my longest aging process to date."

I stood, frozen. I was only three or four steps away from where he stood at his makeshift podium, but he felt a million miles away and my feet felt too heavy to take me to him.

"Remle?" He waived his hand, inviting me to stand next to him. With a gentle shove from Meadow who stood just behind me, I crossed the small expanse, into his waiting embrace.

"This bottle has a special name. Vivaha."

Off somewhere behind me I heard someone gasp. In all the chatter and noise I thought how odd it was I heard it.

"In Hindu culture, a Vivaha is a sacred union. One that is made between a man and a woman when they pledge to love and support one another for eternity. In twenty-five years, I want to be able to open this bottle, on our anniversary and look back and what an amazing life we've had together, and toast all of the blessings we've yet to experience. Because, Remle Clay, I want nothing more than to have you beside me as my life's partner."

"Of course."

I could barely choke out those two words around the

swell of emotion fighting to also break free. I looked from my family to his, all of our friends reflecting on how much can happen in a year. I was going to be Mrs. Remle Raj, new resident of North Carolina, and entrepreneur.

"I wanted to get something as unique and stunning as the amazing woman who would wear it," Jasper continued. The ring was like nothing I'd ever seen. A stunning peacock blue diamond, set with diamond filigrees.

"When I saw this stone it reminded me of you in so many ways," he continued, "from your expressive eyes to the university you love so much, you wear a practically threadbare T-shirt to bed every night." He winked at me with heat in his eyes.

"But what this stone reminds me most, is that sometimes the solution for a rainstorm, is the sun bursting through, demanding to be seen. From today on, you are my forever sunshine."

What a year, indeed. While pursuing Jasper Raj had started as a professional pursuit, finding him changed my life. He taught me about taking risks fearlessly, how passion comes in many forms and every single one of them has the most satisfying rewards. From now until the chapter closed on our life story together, we'd toast all the ways in which a little *whiskey business* brought us together.

willow's mea culpa

HELLO I'M
Mea Culpa

For those who have read me before, you know that I use my mea culpa to admit/acknowledge/accept all of the shit that I took serious creative license on in my book. As a reminder this is a literal last minute brain dump thrown into the back of the book just before I hit publish—so there's probably going to be typos. No one sees this but me.

First and foremost, as always I want to extend my gratitude to you for spending your pennies on my book.

So you may or may not have seen the dedication to this book. Yes. I actually have a friend named Jasper. Years ago, he and I worked together I think I only had two books published when we were coworkers. And in the middle of discussion about who knows what he asked me why there were never any Indian guys in romance novels. That it was always chesty white guys on the cover and he said something to the effect of —we have the Kama Sutra, clearly we'd be awesome lovers. Fast forward to this opportunity and I decided it was time for Jasper's suggestion to be born. And, what better way than to honor the person who prompted the story than to name my main character after him (his last name is not Raj).

If you read Codename: Dustoff, you sort of met Jasper for a half second in that one. That book is also where Amelia is introduced (Emmett's girlfriend), and you get a revisit from Finn, Gemini, and of course Emmett.

That series begins with Beard on Tap which is where you'll learn about Finn and Gemini's story. You also meet Penn Ellis whose story begins in Bed of Roses continues through Independence Bae and even more in Date and Switch which has no preorder yet. Date and Switch is Bryce Ellis' story (he was in this one briefly).

You also meet Sawyer Bennett, whom you might have just met last month in Deck Pic. If you don't follow me on Amazon or subscribe to my newsletter, you might want to. I have so many stories coming out this year and they all intermingle.

Okay to the Mea Culpas...

1. First I realized that I've become obsessed lately with tattoos written in Latin. IDK why. Jasper has one, Sawyer has one, I think Bryce might even have one. I'm not sure why suddenly everyone has become super esoteric with their ink. I did take Latin in HS and college but... not sure why suddenly twenty plus years later it's come to the forefront of my mind. Maybe because I dig intellectual men. Anyhow, yes I do see the pattern, haha.

2. So, the National Bourbon Association is made up. Kentucky has a bourbon association specifically to Kentucky but there isn't anything on the national scale that I could find.

3. Bourbon is still pretty exclusive to Kentucky. In order for a spirit to be considered bourbon it *should* be distilled

in Kentucky. While the internets don't agree on this, I have yet to see a bourbon NOT come from Kentucky. But its possible, supposedly. Someone might prove me wrong and be like hey there's xyz company in whatever state.

4. All bourbon tastes, flavor profiles etc are from #SIROTI (shit I researched on the internet if you're new to me). If you blindfolded me and asked me to taste test five bourbons I would not have any clue how to tell them apart. I know that's bourbon blasphemy. I'm just not a big drinker.

5. There actually IS a bourbon trail but its exclusive to Kentucky.

Fun fact— I'm a Kentucky Colonel—long boring story on how I became one, but each year over Veteran's day is Colonel's weekend in Louisville—where you spend a day at Churchill Downs, and another on the Bourbon trail. And when you get to Buffalo Trace and rumors of a new Pappy being bottled you would honestly think they were selling a hundred dollar big screen tvs at Walmart.

Also, I'm not trying to throw shade at anyone from Kentucky, who works in Bourbon distilling or who went to UK. I loved the thought of someone in a different state wanting to be a bourbon and the people in Kentucky being like sorry you're not bourbon and examining that tension as told through a love story.

6. The premise of each of the stories in this collaboration was that they're written around a specific holiday. My publishing schedule this year had me picking a June date because Im overcommitted for most of this year and have bananas xmas stories Ive signed up for. Anyhow, other than Father's day which I hate secret baby tropes and the kinds of story lines that one would use for a Father's Day holiday are not ones I typically write in. So I saw June 14th was Bourbon

Appreciation Day and I was like ohhhh what if I had someone who distilled in Whiskey country but he was technically by all accounts bourbon. And, what if he was more of a hobbyist distiller that suddenly blew up and became a really well known distiller — and he's good at distilling because he's really smart and sciency. But why would he be sciency—I know because he's a doctor who had to take all those super hard classes I categorically avoided in college because I don't math and most of the sciences require math. And so then the line of the shattered doctor came about.

7. I wrote Jasper as a character with love. While the actual Jasper did not read this book prior to publish my friend Zeenia Patel did act as my consultant and to her I am eternally grateful. India is a very large country, and I am in no way attempting to paint with a single broad stroke an entire culture. I simply wanted to provide a hero that isn't the cookie cutter of what you see in romance.

8. So apparently this is the book for borrowing names from friends. Remle Clay is actually two borrowed names. One of my friends from high school named her daughter Remle and I thought wow what a beautiful and unusual name. She was named after my friends grandpa, Elmer, so that is actually a true story but it doesn't belong to me, it belongs to my friend Amanda. I also went to high school with a descendant of the Clay family of Kentucky. *That* Clay. Henry Clay—the Civil War Clays. She would tell literally anyone with two ears that she was a descendant of *those* Clays. She and I weren't really ever friends—and I'm not even connected with her on Facebook so I have no idea if she still tells people she's one of those Clays... but anyhow when

trying to find a last name for Remle—Clay just seemed to roll off the tongue nicely.

But MY Remle Clay is not a descendant of *those* Clays. She's just a regular old normal person with a nice sounding name.

9. I took a LOT of creative liberties on the E.R. and Jasper's dead patient. Like a LOT. Please don't come at me. It's a romance novel, not a medical guide on life saving procedures. I know every ER doctor and nurse is going to be like "that would never happen" Without pulling myself too far into the weeds with what happens when someone dies and when they extract organs for donations — I literally had no idea in my #SIROTI that they keep you medically sustained while they take your organs. I'm not going to get into the gory details but I went down a black hole about organ harvesting and yeah... I would have never survived medical school (once a long time ago I thought it would be cool to be a pediatrician).. A shift in the ER would have killed me. Legit.

ANYHOW— I tried to put myself in the shoes of the doctors and nurses that are awake for bananas amounts of hours in tragedies or natural events when new shifts can't reach them to relieve them. And how after a while when you're really tired your mind starts to play tricks on you. And what would happen if a doctor and a nurse declare a patient medically dead but either just in the natural process of a body dying or a trick of the mind, one of them thought the patient was in fact still alive and able to be saved and the other one was like no way they're gone and we need to make this split second decision to get the team in here so that they can actually utilize these organs before they too start to (I can't remember the medical term they used in all my research—essentially when they stop receiving oxygenated blood and they too start to die)

So that was where my train of thought was. I know there's probably a million things incorrect. I used #SIROTI to inform my story—and I'm sure unless I was actually a medical student or a doctor most of these events are a cascade of split decisions based on really smart people using science. I am in awe of every doctor and nurse, seriously, because you do the hard things that I would never be able to do.

I just badly write scenarios that have probably have you twitching, But know I do it with respect and admiration.

Also apologies if I misunderstood humanitarian physician practices and whether or not volunteering at a free clinic would fall under the same umbrella as say, a Doctors Without Borders

10. If you live in a state or area where you're like there's no way that a city could get that much snow in one period. Oh contraire ...

Snowmageddon (2011) The snow fell so fast and so hard that people literally got stranded on Lake Shore Drive... to the point that their cars ran out of gas and they had to walk (in a blizzard) to the condos along LSD and hope someone would be kind and take them in (or they slept in the lobbies of the condos and people brought pillows and blankets and food and cell phone charges down for them to use) It was B A N A N A S

Snowpocalypse (2015)

So as I've said in all my other releases this month I planned horribly. A lot of these collaborations are a year in the making, and 🎵 *I'm just a girl who can't say no* 🎵 so suddenly

I found myself drowning in deadlines. I have the summer to kind of find my bearings again. I have quite a few books coming out in fall, so Oy. Why did I think this was a good idea, haha.

Flirt Like a Champ- August 19

Secret Santa (A Curvy Christmas)

Star of Wonder (A Christmas Anthology SHORT)

Rental Clause

I also have Date and Switch that is sitting on my editor's desk and it got pushed back whileI did all of these other releases so that more than likely will release in fall. I'd say September probably.

As always writing is a very lonely and solitary endeavor. There are so many amazing women in my life that I am so grateful to. To the incomparable Khloe Summers you are the most amazing writing friend a girl can have and I am so lucky to have you in my life. To my Arizona writing tribe: Rebecca Gallo, Tara Carr and Ruthie Henricks, thank you for always being a message away.

To Amy Briggs my editor. Y'all writing seriously messes with your head. Especially because writing opens you up to a lot of criticism. I swear every book I send to Amy I'm like "this is the one she's going to email me back and say 'Willow, you're shit. I suggest you not publish this because you're worthless and a terrible story teller." She never does, thank God. Haha. And she is literally the very best cheerleader. Over the years she and I have become great friends as well as my editor and I appreciate the hell out of her.

Being vulnerable is hard and scary as hell—but she manages to soothe all of those doubt monsters and imposter syndrome drumbeats out of my head, and I for that she deserves all the gratitude and a hell of a lot of coffee because I've really tested the limits of her abilities rapid releasing this year haha. My meme sharer, fellow grammarian and member of the oxford comma society—I am incredibly lucky to call you my friend.

To Deb the most amazing beta in the world, I am forever grateful for you, your motivation an encouragement.

To Andi Lynne I don't deserve you but I'm gonna hold on tight regardless. You are my favorite and there's no one I'd rather do a mimosa Sunday with, than you. I love you infinity.

To my unicorn squad life has been B A N A N A S this first six months of 2022. You are always in my heart and I cherish every second I get to spend with you—even if we have to schedule it months out and then reschedule it six times before we finally can get together. You are the best girl squad I could ever ask for. I will always enthusiastically clap for you.

I think that's it for this iteration of Mea Culpas. I always say "this is going to be short"...and then it's not haha. Anyhow keep scrolling to see the list of others in this series and keep scrolling past that to see my upcoming books!

get plundered with sawyer & wren

Sawyer

As a kid I always wanted to be an FBI agent. It was probably because of all those action movies with the guy with the government issued shoes and the shiny blue windbreaker shouting "FBI! Don't Move!" that sucked me in. Number of times I've worn a shiny blue windbreaker or shouted F-B-I? None. Instead of breaking down physical doors, I open virtual ones. Some of the world's most notorious hackers were taken down by my team.

Nighthawk, the notorious Robin hood hacker, evaded everyone. It was up to my team to find this modern day pirate, and take them down. Life on a mega yacht pretending to be a billionaire? I thought it would be a cake walk, until Wren Freidman walked onto my yacht. She'd been hired to fix our comms station, but I found myself searching for excuses to keep talking to her.

Nighthawk needed to be brought to justice. I needed to focus on uncovering his identity, yet the only thing I wanted to do was learn more about the woman with the unicorn colored locs and a super computer for a brain.

When the takedown of my career uncovers hidden truths, the pirate's booty could have my career walking the plank.

Deck Pic is a curvy heroine, modern day pirate, instalove. Guaranteed safe with no cheating and no cliffhangers! Why not spend some time swabbing me deck!

be wooed by anders & phoebe

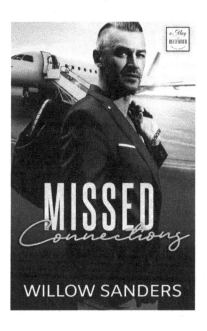

♥ Phoebe ♥

No one expects to meet their Prince Charming sitting on an airplane, least of all me. But there he is. Anders is charming and funny and completely rocks the "I'm a sexy Viking who just crawled out of bed" look. By the time we land in England, I'm pretty well smitten. Still, I'm here for work and not romance. But when we meet again where I'll be doing my research, I'm convinced we just might be fate.

♦ Anders ♦

There is not a person alive who would understand me being tired of the royal life. I've never wanted to be a prince, but I never resented my commitments more than when I met Phoebe. She's everything I could want; curvy, intelligent and honest. I'm determined to make her fall in love with me before she discovers the secrets that could destroy us both.

about the author

You can stalk me at all the links below BUT most of the fun is being had over on TIKTOK. Legit. Come stalk me there.

about the author

You can stalk me at all the links below BUT most of the fun is being had over on TIKTOK Legit. Come stalk me there.

Lightning Source UK Ltd.
Milton Keynes UK
UKHW040952170223
417088UK00004B/89